Pieces of Georgia

a novel

JEN BRYANT

A YEARLING BOOK

For—
Leigh, Jeffrey, Rachel, Michael, Maddie Jo, and Miles . . .
and for young artists everywhere

Published by Yearling, an imprint of Random House Children's Books
a division of Random House, Inc., New York

Yearling and the jumping horse design are registered trademarks of Random House, Inc.

Visit us on the Web! www.randomhouse.com/kids

Educators and librarians, for a variety of teaching tools, visit us at
www.randomhouse.com/teachers

ISBN: 978-0-440-42055-2

Reprinted by arrangement with Alfred A. Knopf Books for Young Readers

Printed in the United States of America

November 2007

10 9 8 7 6 5

First Yearling Edition

"*Live* your life. *Write* your life. *Paint* your life . . .

very few people do that. They're scared of it."

—Andrew Wyeth

part I

"I was a rather silent child."

—Jamie Wyeth

I.

Mrs. Yocum called me
down to her office today. She's the counselor at school who I
have to go to once a week 'cause I'm on
some "At Risk" list that I saw once on the secretary's desk.
(Ronnie Kline, Marianne Ferlinghetti, Sam Katzenbach,
Danita Brown—and some others I forget—are on it, too.)
Most of them have *substance abuse* next to their names,
but I have *financial/single parent—father/possible medical?*
next to mine.

Anyway, when Mrs. Yocum called me in, I sat
in her big green chair, and she sat
across from me in her big blue chair—
blinking at me like a mother owl through her oversize glasses—
and it all started off as it usually does,
with her asking me about my stomachaches
and if I had raised my hand more often in class
and if there was anything particular on my mind I thought
I needed to talk about.

Then all of a sudden she asked me if I
miss you. She never
asked me that before, and I couldn't make the words
come out of my mouth, they seemed to be
stuck in my throat, or maybe they were just tangled up
with the rabbit I seemed to have swallowed

that started kicking the sides of my stomach,
desperate to get out.

I guess it must have been four or five minutes we sat there,
her making notes in her folder
and me with that rabbit
thrashing around my insides and still no
words coming out.

I started to draw on the top of my binder,
like it seems I always do
when I don't know what else to do, so I
didn't notice that she was trying to hand me
a red leather notebook (this very one I'm writing in),
and she said: "Georgia, why don't we make
a deal? I will excuse you
from coming to Guidance for a while, *provided*—
you promise to write down your thoughts and feelings
at least a few times a week
in this diary. You don't have to show it to me, or to anybody,
unless you want to,
and it might be a good idea if you tried—sometimes, or
all the time if you want—
to write down what you might tell, or what you might ask,
your mother
if she were here."

So, Momma, that's how I've come to start
writing to you in this pretty red leather diary
that I keep in the drawer of my nightstand.
But I'm not sure what I'm going to tell you, 'cause my life
is not all that interesting, but anyway
it will fill
a few minutes after school
or maybe that half hour or so
after dinner, after homework, after doing the dishes,
when I'm stretched out in the back of our trailer and Daddy
is trying to keep the TV down so I can fall asleep
but loud enough so he can still watch
whatever game is on
and I'm trying to remember what it was like six years ago
when we were a family
and Daddy was happy
and you were here.

2.

Today I turned thirteen.
As usual for mid-February, it snowed a little bit, then the
sun came out like a tease, 'cause it never got above
thirty-two degrees.

As usual, it was just me and Daddy having my birthday dinner
at the fold-down table in the kitchen.
I said I could make chicken, baked potatoes, and peas,
but he brought home a pizza after work
(with anchovies and green peppers)
and we ate it right out of the box so it'd stay hot,
'cause it wouldn't fit inside our oven.

Then Daddy carried in a cake
he'd been hiding in the closet, but when he
uncovered it, he got mad
because a heat vent was right next to it
and the icing around the edges melted
and the "Happy Birthday" ran all
over the middle until it looked like
a big pink puddle.

But I didn't mind. Last year
he forgot my birthday altogether until
he saw the mail and the annual
$20 bill from Great-Uncle Doug in Atlanta.

The cake was good—chocolate with chocolate icing.
I had seconds and Daddy did, too, and I know
you would've joined us.

Afterward, I went through the mail and I
got a card and the $20 bill from Great-Uncle Doug.
The card had a clown and balloons and was really made
for a little kid, but still,
it was nice of him to remember.

Daddy gave me those jeans I'd seen in the Army Navy Store,
a new pair of shoes,
and a "blank inside" card like he always does,
one with a flower on the front, same as always,
and his big, slanted lettering inside:

   Georgia—

     Happy Birthday.

      Daddy

Can I tell you something, Momma?

Every year since you died, I've been waiting for him
to write *Love, Daddy* inside,
but after all this time
I think I should wake up and stop
my dreaming.

3.

Today when the bus let me off at the end of the lane,
I pulled the mail out of the split
wooden box that says "Kesey/McCoy"
and still has the "19 Slipstream Road" I painted on it
when The Oaks development went up beside us
and all of a sudden
even those of us who'd been here for years
got assigned new numbers. (We still live in our same trailer,
but not long after you died, Daddy decided
to move us out of the trailer park,
where there were lots of good people but also
a few of the other kind. Now we live on a sixty-acre horse farm
near Longwood, where it's a lot safer for me
to stay alone when he's working.)

Anyway, in the mailbox there was a long cream-colored
envelope addressed to *Miss Georgia McCoy*
and up in the left-hand corner, in dark brown ink:
The Brandywine River Museum, Route 1, Chadds Ford, PA 19317.

I thought maybe it was
a mistake. Not counting Great-Uncle Doug's birthday card
and the postcard I get every August from school
with my new bus number on it, I get exactly
zero mail. But there was nothing else
written on it. I flipped it over a few times, read

my name and address again, then
opened it.

Inside, there was this strange
formal letter, all typed up and neat, that said:

Dear Miss McCoy:

Enclosed please find your annual membership card,
which entitles you to all privileges listed below
and which expires one year from date of purchase.

The letter said I was entitled to
free admission anytime the museum was open, plus
"a ten percent discount to the museum shop."

At the bottom, it said:
This Brandywine gift is from: _____
And on that blank line, someone had typed
anonymous.

I put it in my backpack, but all afternoon,
while I took Blake for a long run in the field,
and walked up to buy milk and cereal at the convenience store,
and watched Mr. Fitz, one of the horse boarders, try to
catch his mare in the pasture, and started to look up
stuff on the computer for my English paper,
I kept wondering who
anonymous was.

Well, it's surely not Daddy. He won't talk about
my sketching and drawing. He doesn't try
to stop me or anything, but I can tell
he wishes I'd find something else I like to do better.
After all this time, Momma, he still doesn't like anything
that reminds him
of you.

It's not my art teacher, Miss Benedetto. Teachers aren't allowed
to give gifts to students.

There's Great-Uncle Doug in Atlanta. I've never met him,
but you told me once how you were his
favorite niece (I imagine him tall and slim
with a slow smile and big blue eyes).
But I don't think he knows I like to draw, or anything at all about me,
and anyway, he already
sent my birthday money.

I don't have any other relatives except
your folks,
who have never sent me anything,
and I suppose they don't even know
where we live.

I was going to show the letter to Daddy before dinner, but he was
worn-out when he got home. He and his crew
are working at a new construction site out in Lancaster County.
He leaves about 5:30 in the morning

and doesn't get back until 7:00 at night. He says
the houses are selling as fast as they can build them,
and with spring coming,
they're putting them up quick.

He brought me a photo of the model home,
and I could not believe
how *huge* it was. It was even bigger than
my friend Tiffany's house. (She lives in the development
next to us, where the houses are large enough for four families
and you have to be real careful you go into
your own front door 'cause each house
has the same driveway, the same lawn, the same
scraggly trees out front,
and mostly the same kinds of cars in the garage.)

Daddy and me—we don't
talk much anyway, but when he's that tired, we
hardly talk at all.
It's not that we don't get along. I mean, we don't
fight or anything. But you know how quiet Daddy was even
when you were here?
Well, he's even quieter now.
And since I've started growing up a little, you know,
"exhibiting the early signs of puberty"
(that's straight out of our seventh-grade health book, page 33),
it's like suddenly I'm from a different country
even though we've been living in this little trailer,

just the two of us—
and your crazy dog, Blake, of course—
for the past six years.
Anyway, I decided it was not a good night
to bring up that membership. I'm gonna wait
until tomorrow—I'm sure that'll be
a much better time.

4.

In art class, we saw slides
of oil paintings by Georgia O'Keeffe. Miss Benedetto told us
how the artist grew up on a farm in Wisconsin
and then moved to Virginia
(and later her mother died there, too)
and then to Texas, where she fell in love with
all that open space (she especially loved the thunderstorms),
and then to New York, where she painted the Hudson River
and skyscrapers as dark and tall as canyon walls,
but the place she loved best
was the wide, dry desert and red clay hills
of New Mexico.

Most of the slides were of flowers—really big ones—
like lilies and peonies and orchids.
Michael Stitt, who sits behind me,
kept whispering about the center of the flowers looking like
our health class handouts for "The Male Anatomy,"
and everybody started giggling until Miss Benedetto told him
he'd have to stay in for detention
and draw some just like that
unless he shut up fast.
I thought the flowers were good, but I liked
the bone paintings best. All those skulls and hips and ribs—
she painted them so smooth and clean, it made me
want to touch them.

Miss B. let us look at a bunch of Georgia O'Keeffe books
that she brought from home
with more paintings of monster-size flowers,
bones and skulls, and sometimes flowers and bones together.
There was one of a cow's skull
that reminded me of a page in your sketchbook—
the one with your name, Tamara Speare,
stamped in gold on the front—
that Daddy keeps in his truck.

There was another picture, of black pears in a bowl,
and one of a cottonwood tree,
and I know you sketched those, too.

All this time I thought you and Daddy named me
for the state you were both born and raised in,
but when I looked in those books
and remembered your sketches, I wondered

if maybe you named me Georgia
for the artist who painted flowers and bones
so that you see them fresh,
like they are secret worlds you can lose yourself inside
if the real one gets too bad.

Momma, I am sure
that's the very first thing I'd ask,
if you were here.

5.

The Oaks is the development next to us
where Tiffany lives. The builders named it for
the grove of giant trees that used to grow there before
the bulldozers mowed them down.

Last spring, when Tiffany moved in with her family,
there was no one else in the whole development.
We met by the pond, when she was wandering around
and I was trying to sketch the old icehouse
and the water with the geese drifting
like slow white ghosts among the lilies.

She sat right down next to me and started talking, telling me
all about where she'd lived (five different states,
and for one year in Mexico)
and how she was almost thirteen—
older than most kids in sixth grade—
and how she was going to try out for all the sports teams at school
and asking did I know of any place where she could buy
a new lacrosse stick
and what kind of horses were grazing in the field
and how old was I, and in what grade,
and was the school an easy one or strict
and were any of those horses mine.

I wanted to finish my sketch because it was the third time I'd tried
to draw those geese and they were finally starting

to *look* like geese and not chickens,
but she was jabbering so much, and I didn't want to be rude,
so I told her everything she wanted to know, and especially

that we were both in sixth grade, even though she was older
(she got held back after that year in Mexico),
and that Longwood Middle School was strict in some ways
and easy in others,
and then (I watched her real careful when I said this)
I told her straight out that I lived
only with my daddy, a construction worker, in the trailer,
and we rented that space from Mr. Kesey, who owned the farm,
and that my momma had died
of a one-week pneumonia when I was seven,
and most of the horses belonged to people who didn't live here,
and I earned money cleaning and walking them,
and then I told her I needed to be up at the barn at four o'clock
to groom Ella for Mr. Fitz, and she asked
if she could come, too.
She didn't seem to care that I was almost a whole year younger
or that I wasn't rich
or that I didn't play sports
or have a mother
or nice clothes.

That was a year ago, and Tiffany and me have been friends
ever since.
We ride the same bus, which stops for me at the end of the lane,
and the rest of the kids who have moved in,

they all think I live in the big farmhouse,
and Tiffany has never told them
different.

If you think about it,
it doesn't make much sense that we are friends:
    She's athletic—I'm not.
    She has a regular family (a mother, father, little brother)—
        I just have Daddy.
    She's real popular in school—I'm not.
    She loves to talk—I don't.
    She's Catholic—I don't go to church.
    Her family has lots of money—we just get by.
    Her father works for some company in that big corporate center
        near the turnpike and flies all over the country for meetings.
    He drives a new BMW.
    Mine puts up the walls and nails down the floors
        of the houses that people like Tiffany live in.
    He drives a ten-year-old Ford pickup.

I guess I'm telling you this because Mrs. Yocum told me
to write about the things I might ask you
if you were here. I guess I'd ask you
how two people who are so different
can stay friends. I'd ask you about the friends you had
when you grew up in Savannah.

Tiffany's only in one of my classes
(Mr. Krasinski's math, and he doesn't let us talk),

and her popular jock friends treat me like I'm
invisible. But Tiffany always says hi to me in the halls, and sometimes
she sits with me at lunch (but not always),
and she makes her mother beep the horn
when they drive by on the way to
basketball games, lacrosse matches and practices,
or when she sees me out walking the horses
or tossing tennis balls for the dog.

The truth is, sometimes I worry
about Tiffany. She's always busy.
Sometimes she looks as tired as Daddy
after one of his overtime days. Take
yesterday, for example: She came up to the barn
after lacrosse practice
(at school, it doesn't start till the second week of March,
but Tiffany's real good, so she plays on a club team
that practices indoors in the winter
and competes in tournaments all year).

I was grooming Ella, and the other horses were all
in their stalls with their blankets on,
munching sweet feed and corn,
and the mother cat was nursing her newborn kittens.
Tiffany brushed the snow off her sneakers, plopped herself
down on a hay bale, and before we started to talk—
her back propped straight up against the wall—
she fell asleep.

6.

When my best friend Tina moved to Cleveland
at the end of fifth grade, it was
the second-worst thing
that ever happened.

You didn't know Tina (we became
best friends in third grade, the year after you died),
but we were the same
in many ways. . . . Her real father died when she was five,
and she lived in a tiny apartment over the 7-Eleven
with her mother and younger brother.
Tina loved to draw as much as I do, so we'd spend
part of every weekend
lying on her mother's old sheepskin in the living room,
our colored pencils scattered everywhere,
making pictures of our pets
and the kids we knew from school.

But then Tina's mother got remarried. Tina's stepdad
worked at a car parts factory in Philadelphia
that shut down
and relocated all of its workers
to Ohio.

I wrote to her for a while, and she wrote back,
but then I stopped.

It hurt too much to hear how she had
a new house,
a new school (that she really liked),
and her own pony (Slim Jim) in the yard.

After that, I didn't try to make new friends.
After that, except for Blake and Ella,
I stayed pretty much to myself.

Then along came Tiffany, like a small hurricane,
and somehow we clicked.
We are not the same kind of friends
as me and Tina were—
Tina was more like my twin—
she liked almost everything I liked,
and her family was poor,
and her home was small and plain,
and, for a while, she had only one parent. . . .

Me and Tiffany are not like that—
we come from really different families, and we don't
have a lot in common,
but for some strange reason that I can't explain,
we get along just fine.

7.

Daddy drove right past the Brandywine River Museum
on the way to Delaware. We go just over the state line
every other Saturday to buy food and household supplies
at the grocery. It's a lot cheaper
than anywhere in Pennsylvania, and you don't
have to pay tax. Daddy likes that.
My stomach got all fluttery when we stopped at the red light
on Route 1, right near the entrance and the neat
gray and tan sign that sits out near the side of the road.

I wanted so bad to ask him if we could stop and go in
after we'd done all our errands,
but it felt just like it does when I'm with Mrs. Yocum,
or when Mr. Hendershot asks me a history question
I know the answer to
but I can't make the picture in my head
into the words he wants to hear
and before you know it he's asked someone else
and then my picture disappears.

I still haven't told Daddy about
my getting that anonymous membership. I'm afraid he'll say
I can't go. You know, he still keeps a photo of you
inside your old sketchbook in his truck,
but he turns away whenever I
pick up my own drawing pad and pencil.

I suppose I might be starting
to look more like you did that summer
when he met you at the Savannah College of Art and Design,
when you would sit and draw under those big old magnolias
and he was working construction on one of the dorms
and you asked him to pose for a sketch
because you liked his smile
and he said he would
if you would come with him to dinner. I never
saw that sketch. I'm afraid to ask Daddy
if he still has it.

I was in first grade when you
told me that, remember? I drew a Crayola picture
of a man and a woman standing under a big tree, holding hands
and smiling, and you taped it to our refrigerator.

I imagine you went to art museums in Savannah,
and maybe you even went to some here in Pennsylvania, and maybe
you even went to the Brandywine River Museum.
And if you did, that would be
another reason Daddy wouldn't like me going there,
wouldn't want one more thing to remind him
that right up until the week you died,
what you liked to do best
was dance your pencil across a blank page
and make something come alive.

8.

We got our report cards. There was a
note attached to mine:

Georgia,

I hope you're making time
to write in that diary. You can make
an appointment during school or afterward,
any day but Friday, if you want to talk
about anything at all.

Mrs. Yocum

That was nice, I guess. I still have no idea what she expected
me to say about myself when
we had our little visits. I know my life
is not perfect. I know everyone thinks I'm quiet because
you died. Maybe they're a little bit right.
Maybe I'm naturally shy, like Daddy.
But that doesn't mean I need to be on some "At Risk" list
like it's a sure thing I'm going to start hanging out behind
the Acme to sniff glue with Danita and Sam,
or go smoking with Marianne and her friends,
or steal stuff from the mall with Ronnie.
I mean, what exactly
have I *done* to get my name on that list? Absolutely
nothing, as far as I can tell.

Truth is, I don't know why I'm not more bad than I am,
or why I'm not hanging out with them.
Lord knows I have plenty of time after school,
without Daddy here,
to go anywhere I want and find
some trouble. It's just that I don't mind spending my free time
hot-walking horses or playing with Blake
or just sitting down by the pond,
watching the geese and frogs, being still
and thinking. When I'm bored, my hands always seem to find
a pencil or a piece of charcoal
(Miss Benedetto gives me the old ones
'cause the school orders new boxes every three months
whether she needs them or not), and before I know it,
it's an hour or two later and I have to
set the table, make dinner, and start my homework.

In case you want to know,
I'm not the smartest in seventh grade,
but I do all right. I do what I have to do
to get by.
This time I got three C's, two B's, and one A (in art, of course).
But I'm smart enough to know I don't want to live
in this trailer forever, and since I don't seem to have
a lot of family looking out after me, I'll have to make my own way
in this world someday.
I figure I'll need to graduate high school and maybe go to
community college at least.

Daddy and I have not really
talked about it, but we'll have to soon 'cause he has to sign off
on my course forms for eighth grade
(that's when Mrs. Yocum says
I should start to take certain science and math classes
if I plan on going to college).
The last time we sat down to talk about school,
I needed his permission to see the seventh-grade health film
When You Become a Woman. I watched him
read over the letter that was printed on pink
paper and sign the bottom with his
big tan left hand, which the pen almost disappeared in, and then
I watched him try to say something about it to me,
but it was for him—I'm pretty sure—like it was for me
in Mrs. Yocum's office
when I had that rabbit kicking around my insides
and the words got stuck in my throat.
Daddy had to go outside and have a cigarette, and when he
came back in, he said: "If you have
any questions after that movie, you can ask me,"
but even though that's what his words said, his face said:
"I sure hope you don't have any questions, Georgia."

And do you know what? Just two days after we watched
that stupid film in the gym (Tiffany had already shown me
a book she took from her parents' room,
so I had a pretty good idea where all the parts were
and what they were for), I was in the nurse's office
asking her for sanitary pads.

But lucky for me, Mrs. Reed is just about the best person
in all of Longwood Middle School. She knows
I get those awful stomachaches and keeps
a big bottle of Rolaids, fruit-flavored, just for me.
She asks only what she has to ask
to fill out the forms that get sent to Guidance,
and mostly she just lets me relax on her couch
whenever I'm feeling bad.
You know, I don't even think it's the Rolaids
that make me better. I think it's just a few minutes of lying
down and being quiet, staring at the fishbowl on her desk
and knowing
she's not going to send me back to class
until I'm ready.

Anyway, Mrs. Reed gave me these coupons I can use
to buy my own supplies at the store
and asked me if I had any questions,
just like Daddy did. But her face and her words
matched up, so I asked her
three or four things I wasn't sure about,
and she answered me, patiently, like she wasn't the school nurse,
but almost like I know you would
if you were here.

9.

"My science teacher says people don't
die of pneumonia anymore."

That's what Tiffany said when she
came up to me in the hall right after biology.
She said it casual, like you might say "It was cloudy today,"
like it was something no one could argue.

I stood there while she hauled up her black hair
into the usual ponytail.
She was wearing three-inch heels,
which made her taller than most of the teachers
and *way* taller than me.

"True," I said, tilting my neck back
more than I usually did.
"Most people don't. But my momma was born
with a weakness in her lungs,
and she had to take this special medicine her whole life,
and she basically hated doctors
on account of having to be around them so much as a kid."

I kicked my locker closed and started walking to lunch.
"When Momma got sick, she and Daddy were
saving up for a house," I told Tiffany, offering to split
my bag of Cheese Nips.

"A doctor's appointment would cost,
and Momma kept telling Daddy it was just
a bad flu, like a lot of folks got that winter."

Tiffany took the Cheese Nips and gave me
her bite-size Milky Way. She looked sorry
for bringing up the subject.
But it was okay—
it felt good, in a strange sort of way,
to talk about it.

Early dismissal today. I was home at 1:05,
an hour and a half earlier than usual. Mr. Fitz's horse, Ella,
followed me up the lane, and as I passed
the last gate at the top of the pasture,
she whinnied at me so pathetically, I dropped
my backpack and went inside.

We have this game where I hide a treat in one of my pockets
and she has to do a few tricks for me
before I let her find it. I've taught her to nod yes,
count to six (sometimes she paws the ground, sometimes
she stomps, but I give her credit for either),
and shake all over
like she's a dog just come out of a river. She can also laugh
(she lifts her upper lip and waves it around),
but we're still working on that one.

You know, I think it's a good thing that Ella has me
to see that she's more than just
an animal with good bloodlines,
more than a ribbon-winning jumper, something to show off
to the crowd on Sundays. Today, when I watched her
race around the pasture in the powdery snow
just for the fun of it,
or in the summer when she
rolls in the mud after a hard rain,

or splashes her hoof in the trough 'cause she likes the sound,
I know that's when she's happiest.

Of all the horses that have boarded here,
Ella is the smartest and the sweetest, and Mr. Fitz
doesn't even know it, and probably
doesn't care.

I took Blake for a long walk after school.
We're lucky that your dog is real healthy
and has to go to the vet only for his annual exam.
(We use the SPCA community clinic. It costs just twelve dollars
and they give us free heartworm medicine
and flea powder for a year.) Once in a while he tries
to get Daddy to play,
but like everything else that reminds him of you,
Daddy mostly ignores him.

Blake just turned ten—that's seventy in dog years, I think—
but he's still high-strung. He drives Daddy
crazy at night, whining and pacing
if he doesn't get enough time outside. He doesn't bark much,
and he's stopped chasing Mr. Kesey's geese, which is good,
'cause I'm sure Daddy'd make me give him away
if he annoyed our landlord.

I used to dread going out in the cold to take Blake for walks
or to run him in the fields, but lately I don't mind as much
'cause it seems like I'll E-X-P-L-O-D-E
if I stay inside our trailer for more than an hour or so.
Like today, for instance . . . the snow had melted a little,
and there was mud everywhere.
I walked the first half-mile, then I started jogging, and then I ran—
for no good reason, I just ran—

the whole rest of the bridle trail and across
both big pastures and all the way
up the hill. My shoes got soaked, the back of my jacket got
splattered, and my leg muscles ached.
But I felt so much better—like the wind and mud
had sucked out some of my restlessness.

Whenever I get like this, when I feel like I
just drank twelve cherry Cokes, or like the top of my head
will pop off at any moment,
I start thinking something's wrong with me.
Once, I asked Mrs. Reed about it. She said:
"Georgia, I think you're a pretty normal seventh grader.
All those hormones swooshing through your body
will make you moody,
but don't you worry too much about it."

That made me feel okay . . . for about a day.
And lately when I get to feeling that way,
I put Blake on a leash and just get *out*.
If it's not too muddy, we head over to Tiffany's
(Mrs. O'Neill's real picky about her driveway
getting paw prints on it).
But she's hardly ever home. She's usually at
basketball practice, lacrosse practice, or religious classes.

Last year, at one of her lacrosse games,
she got tripped and fell on her wrist.

She broke it in two places and had to have
an operation to set it straight. Then she got an infection
and had to stay in the hospital for a whole week.

You'd think with all the sports she plays
an injury would make her miserable.
But when I visited her,
she said it was the first time in months she'd had a rest.
"I'm gonna *enjoy* this," she told me.
"The food's no worse than what I usually have after practice,
and there's no coach, no sprints or laps.
It's like those hotels we stay in with my travel team,
but I have unlimited cable TV,
and I can stay up late 'cause I don't have to play
in a tournament early the next day."

We played cards (one-handed War—
I played one-handed, too, so it'd be fair)
and did crossword puzzles and watched
the Hitchcock Film Festival on HBO.

Tiffany got more thoughtful
while she was laid up.
"Maybe I'll quit the summer swim team, or maybe
I'll play only one sport and take up horseback riding just for fun,"
she said while we were watching *Psycho* for the third time,
and I reminded her that she was only
the fastest backstroker in the county

and the star guard on the school basketball team
and maybe she'd feel different after she
laid around a while longer. To cheer her up,
I told her *I* wouldn't mind
having enough money to pay for

a pool membership,
a lacrosse stick and uniform,
a new pair of Nikes, a backboard and hoop,

and I sure wouldn't mind traveling
all over the state on Saturdays,
instead of cutting coupons and food shopping all morning,
and spending the afternoon bathing and braiding
other people's horses for the Sunday shows.

Tiffany just looked at me, and we both
laughed, remembering when she tried to teach me how
to catch and throw a lacrosse ball
and how I accidentally cracked her mother's kitchen window
and how, when we went swimming at her country club,
I swam back and forth across the lanes
instead of up and down.
"I think you are a lot less dangerous
with a sketch pad and pencil," she said,
and I had to agree.

12.

From our trailer, it's a ten-minute walk
to the little shopping center
where the Route I shuttle bus comes.
If I get on and ride three stops, I can get off right
at the traffic light by the
Brandywine River Museum.

Whoever sent me the membership
also sent me this schedule: *Open 9:30 a.m. to 4:30 p.m. daily,
Closed Christmas Day,* and a brochure about its history,
which I've already read five times.
I also looked at their Web site
and at a book in the school library
while I was supposed to be
researching cell division for science.

So far, this is what I know:
The building used to be an old mill and sits
right on the riverbank.
A lot of the stuff inside was painted by three guys
from the same family, all named Wyeth.
The grandfather, N. C. Wyeth, was the oldest.
He was a famous illustrator who painted
pictures for adventure books like *Kidnapped* and *Treasure Island.*
The Web site said he and his wife had five kids
and he encouraged them all to be creative.

His youngest kid was Andrew,
and I think he must be famous, too,
'cause the Web site had links to articles about him in
the *New York Times* and the *Washington Post.*

But Andrew's paintings are a lot different from his father's.
He doesn't use a lot of color, and he doesn't
always paint people
(N. C.'s illustrations almost *always* have people).
Andrew seems more obsessed with the land—
streams and fences, fallen logs and branches, patches of half-
melted snow and dry grass.
You'd think they'd be boring, but each one
is a little mysterious, like something had just happened,
or is about to happen.

Andrew's son James (they call him Jamie)
paints portraits of people
(the one in the book was of President Kennedy—
he looked real serious, but it was good, I thought)
and also portraits of animals: One was a big pink pig
and another was a huge raven,
but Mrs. McGiven caught me
not doing my science, so I had to put the book
back before I could see more.

I'd rather not go to the museum alone, at least not the first time.
I considered telling Tiffany about my anonymous gift,

then asking her to come with me.
But I know she has basketball practice and then lacrosse
and then she has to write an essay for American history
that was due last Friday, when she was
away at a tournament. And anyway, Tiffany has been so
jittery lately, I'm not sure she'd stand still long enough
to actually see the paintings.

I'd take Blake, but they
don't allow pets.

So I guess I'll go by myself, after all.
Tomorrow. Right after school.
This is one of those times, Momma, I really do wish
you were here.

part 2

"When I get an idea that means a lot to me,

I just bury myself in it."

—Andrew Wyeth

13.

I got the last seat on the shuttle, way in the back,
where there are no windows. I couldn't see past
the two fat ladies in front of me, so I had no idea
where we were. I would have missed my stop
if the driver hadn't turned around and said:
"Honey, didn't you mean to get off here?"
I thanked her and made sure my watch was set
the same as her clock
so I'd catch the last ride back.

It was a short walk past the gray and tan
sign by the highway
and into the gravel driveway leading to the museum.
My hands were shaking and my stomach
was flip-flopping when I showed my membership card
to the lady in the booth.
She nodded and pointed through the cobblestone courtyard
to the brick steps that fanned out like a skirt
below the entrance.

Unless you took me to one when I was little—
and if you did, I don't remember it—this was my first visit
to an art museum. Miss Benedetto tried to take us
to the Philadelphia Museum of Art,
but when one of the seventh-grade mothers discovered
they had a show on Michelangelo that included nudes,

the PTA made us go
to a paint factory instead.

The guard inside the entrance looked at me hard.
I guess he saw I was new. . . . He walked over to the table
marked "Admissions Desk" and brought me
a map and a floor plan.

He led me upstairs and through a hall that's all
glass on one side and you feel like you could stride right out
over the Brandywine River. At the first room,
he smiled, nodded, and left me
alone. I liked that. Right away I liked that
no one was going to follow me around like I was some
bad kid who shouldn't be there.

I *was* a little nervous—
the people I've seen in pictures of art museums always have
nice clothes and shoes
and they look like they *know* something.
But once I started looking at the paintings and reading
the little white signs next to them on the wall,
I didn't feel nervous at all.

The upstairs room was full of N. C. Wyeths,
and I saw right away that the photos in the books
did not come close to the real thing. That man loved his
bright colors and he painted *big*. Four framed paintings

of Indians came first
(Mr. Hendershot would say "Native Americans,"
but even the descriptions next to the paintings said "Indians,"
so I guess things were different back then).

In the one called *The Guardians,* three old men in deerskin
are sitting cross-legged on a ridge.
One wears a necklace of bear claws and one
has eagle feathers around his head. The last one has enormous
dark brown hands, like Daddy's, and his shoulders are
draped in skins. They look lean and fit,
like they were chiseled right out of the rock.

Then came one with a long title:
The Children Were Playing at Marriage-by-Capture.
A boy wearing nothing but a thin cloth tied around his hips
is chasing a girl in a deerskin dress as she
leaps over a creek. I counted twenty-five diagonal lines.
(In art class, Miss Benedetto is always making us
draw lines through paintings so we'll "see the geometry."
Of course, I just drew them with my eyes this time.)

On the October Trail (A Navaho Family) was next—
a handsome man on a brown horse, his wife riding beside him
on a donkey, a tiny baby strapped to her back.
What a great view that baby must have had . . .
watching eagles and flocks of hawks,
thunderclouds and the tops of distant mountains.

A single Indian in his canoe, on a wide, foamy river,
steep canyons rising on either side . . .
That one was called *In the Crystal Depths*.
The Indian's oar is still. He's staring down, looking for something—
or maybe he's thinking—or maybe he's admiring his reflection,
like that Narcissus guy we read about in English.
Something about it was sad.

N. C. Wyeth's pirates came next.
These were big paintings, too, and he used lots
of browns, yellows, and blues.
The pirates have nasty faces and some have gold hoop
earrings and head scarves and carry knives.
I wanted to read more about them on the signs,
but it was already after 4:00,
so I had to go.

On the bus ride, I realized I hadn't seen one picture
by Andrew or Jamie Wyeth (there wasn't time!).
I realized that even if I go there right after school,
I will only have an hour or so. But whoever
anonymous is, whoever
gave me that membership, must know that. . . .
so I'll go whenever I can.

The shuttle dropped me back at the shopping center
at quarter till five, and I was inside our trailer
in less than ten minutes. I went right to my

nightstand, pulled out this diary, and started writing, my heart
pounding like a bass drum.

Then Daddy called and said I should go ahead with dinner,
'cause he had to wait for the foreman to sign some papers
and he'd be home sometime after 8:00. I made
my voice sound casual on the phone,
like I'd spent the whole afternoon at home,
doing nothing.

14.

Mr. Krasinski caught me
sketching Indians in the margins
of my math book. He was trying to teach us *x to the third power,*
but all I could think about
were those N. C. Wyeth paintings—
that baby looking at the sky, and that one
lonely guy staring into the river.

Mr. K. made me stay in
for lunch to work on some extra problems. But even then
I kept picturing those three Indian men
sitting on that mountain, that canoe in the canyon,
those Navajo with their donkey and their baby.

Half of my mind was working on *x to the third times twenty,*
while the other half was wondering
if I'll ever have enough money for proper art supplies
and if I will ever find someone to teach me
how to use them. Next year Old Mrs. Finnegan is retiring
and they're hiring
a new art teacher for eighth grade, so I don't know
if the new teacher will give me
charcoal and sketchbooks for free, like Miss B.

Mr. Krasinski corrected my stuff. He said I got enough
right to make up for my not paying attention in class.

"Georgia, I know you prefer to draw, but you're going to have to
deal with numbers your whole life, so I'd
take this class more seriously, if I were you."

He doesn't know that
I *do* think about numbers all the time . . .
at least when it comes to money. I have tried to put aside
some of what I've earned from the horse boarders
for when I'm sixteen and get my license.
Tiffany says in two years, when she's sixteen,
her father's going to give her his blue BMW,
" 'cause by then he'll want a new one in a different color."

I laughed when she told me that.
But when I saw she wasn't kidding,
I almost cried.

15.

I stayed after today 'cause
Tiffany had a play-off basketball game against Pennfield.
It'll be the best one, she wrote on the note she passed in math,
and my father can drive you home when it's done.
She knows I'm not much of a sports fan. . . . I don't really get
all the fuss about strategies and scores,
and after glow-in-the-dark flea collars, I think cheerleaders
are the stupidest things ever invented.

But I *do* like basketball—Daddy is a big 76ers fan,
and I watch their games with him whenever I can. Besides, even if
you're someone who doesn't know squat about sports,
you would see right away
that Tiffany is *good.*

In the first half, she scored fourteen points and had six assists,
and she dribbled around those Pennfield girls so fast,
they looked like they were standing still.
You could see the other team getting frustrated 'cause
nothing they did could stop her—
she shot from way out, or she might drive right into them,
make some impossible layup
and draw the foul. Amazing.
By the end of the game, she had twenty-four points
and I lost count of how many
steals and assists.

I waited outside the locker room,
where I could hear them whooping and hollering
'cause Pennfield is our rival
and we hadn't beaten them in girls' basketball
in seven years. Tiffany came out of there first,
but it didn't look like she'd showered.
I said: "Hey, I can wait—you don't have to rush
just to get me home."
She said: "I've got club lacrosse practice tonight. I'll get
sweaty there anyway."

I have no idea where she gets her energy. She must have
twice as much as most people . . .
which is a good thing, I guess, 'cause most days
she's just getting home
when I've already done my assignments, had dinner,
and crawled into bed.

Her father drove us through McDonald's across from school.
I got a Big Mac and fries, and Tiffany got
a milk shake and Chicken McNuggets, and we crammed
them down in ten minutes.
I helped her do a little math and study for French,
but when we pulled up to the entrance of the indoor
sports complex, she still had twenty problems left
and she knew only two out of thirty French verbs.

It was already 7:30.
I could tell by the slow way she was moving

that Tiffany would rather go home. But she grabbed
her shoes from the back, kissed her dad,
and tapped me on the head with her stick.
"Bye, G. See ya on the bus."

Seeing her then made me think of Ella and how, sometimes,
she walks slow and pulls back on the rope
when Mr. Fitz takes her from the field
and into the riding ring for training.

If Ella were a person
and not a horse,
she would understand Tiffany perfectly.

16.

Remember I told you about that time last year
when Tiffany broke her wrist and got an infection
and had to stay in the hospital?
Well, Momma, by the end of that week she was getting
pretty bored and pretty fidgety.
Her jock friends had stopped visiting,
we'd watched all the game shows on TV, and we'd played
way too many hands of War. So, to keep her mind busy,
I told her the little bit I know about you
and your life in Savannah.

I started with the part about your being
sick a lot when you were young,
how twice you had to stay in the hospital in Atlanta
for some problem with your lungs,
and you took this special medicine most of your life
because of it. I told her that's how you

started drawing—
all those days when you didn't
feel so good and you stayed home in bed,
how Maggie, your mother's maid, dreamed up stories
of tiny people and talking animals
and secret kingdoms under the sea,
and you would sketch the characters and the scenes,
and she'd put them up all around your room

and you'd hold an art show for your dad
when he came home (Tiffany liked that part a lot).

When the nurse came around with a cart
of newspapers and magazines, the only one that seemed
halfway interesting was a back issue of
Modern Bride. We took it and looked through it
together—me flipping the pages slowly and Tiffany's
eyes opening wide at all the exotic places you can go
after you say "I do."

"My mom and dad got married
in St. Patrick's Cathedral in New York," she told me.
"They spent their honeymoon skiing the Alps. . . .
If I ever get married,
I'm going someplace warm, like Hawaii.
We'll rent a yacht and go deep-sea fishing, and then
we'll rent a jeep like you see in those commercials
and drive all around the islands with a guide. . . .
So . . . where do you want to go on your honeymoon?"

I needed a minute to think—it's not a subject I'm used to.
"I've never stayed in a nice hotel before," I replied.
"So pretty much anywhere will be fine."

Tiffany got that pouty look, so I made up something quick.
"But I'd like to go to New York City," I said,
"and visit the museums and the stores and take the

subway to Brooklyn and Queens and go
to see a Broadway show."

She liked that answer better. Then she asked:
"Where were your parents married,
and how did they meet?"

Questions sometimes run off her tongue like water off a cliff,
but she knows I don't always answer
real personal stuff. Maybe it was because I started the subject
in the first place.
Or maybe I just felt sorry for her
with her fracture, and how her other "friends" deserted her.
Whatever it was, I gave in:
"My momma had an older brother who got
killed in a car accident. After that,
she wasn't allowed to go anywhere alone.
Her parents kept her at home
and hardly let her out. I guess they were scared of losing her, too.
It drove Momma crazy, though.
She ran away a couple of times, but she never got too far.
She always came back, usually tired and sick,
saying she was sorry."

Tiffany sat up then a little straighter in her bed.
"Go on. . . ."

"It was her uncle Doug who finally convinced them
that Momma should go to SCAD—

the Savannah College of Art and Design—
so she could earn a degree and meet new people,
and still be close by."

Tiffany leaned forward and scratched under her cast. She really
liked your story, and for some reason
it felt good to tell it. "So did she go?"

Momma, I hope you don't mind. . . . I told her
the rest: how you and Daddy met, how you kept him
a secret for a long time, and when you finally
told them you wanted to marry, they called him
a "poor orphan,"
a "good-for-nothing handyman,"
a "drifter."
They said if you went through with it, then you'd no longer
be their daughter.

Tiffany was really listening now. She
whistled through her teeth. "So they ran off to
Pennsylvania, and had you, and lived in a trailer
until she . . ."

And that's what I like about Tiffany—
she may be pretty careless and even selfish
sometimes, but she knew she shouldn't finish
that sentence.

17.

I've decided when I'm older and I have enough
money saved up, I'm going to go
and see where you were born,
where you grew up,
and where you went to school.

Tiffany and I had library time
together this afternoon, and we looked up
all the places in the 900s section
that we wanted to visit. She looked at books
on the Hawaiian Islands and Africa and I looked at ones
on New Mexico (to see Georgia O'Keeffe's house),
California (no special reason, I just want to see the Pacific Ocean),
and Georgia. There was one called *Unique Georgia*
(Tiffany said that could be the title of my autobiography)
that had a lot of Savannah pictures, and another called
Hidden Georgia with maps of trips you could take
into the countryside.

After school I walked Blake through the fields
and watched this red-tailed hawk
circling and riding the March wind. Then, all of a sudden,
he folded his wings and dove straight down—
I was sure he'd hit the ground—
but at the very end, he swooped up, stretched out his claws,
and grabbed this little sparrow.

It was awful.
That hawk was so deadly, he knew
exactly when to dive
and what to do.

Now I'm sitting on my bed, writing, thinking how
you would understand that poor sparrow. That hawk—
like your one-week pneumonia—
must have come out of nowhere,
and before you could yell for help or do anything at all about it,
it wrapped its claws around you
and carried you off.

18

I thought I knew what a portrait was, but I guess
I don't. Jamie Wyeth (that's the youngest one, Andrew's son)
painted a portrait of his wife, Phyllis,
and all that's in the picture
is a straight-backed chair, some kind of wild, red-berried plant,
and a broad-brimmed hat.

This afternoon, at the museum, I stood and looked at it
for fifteen minutes, wondering why someone would do that.
Then I thought maybe Jamie wanted you to
imagine what his wife was like,
and those were his hints. So, I pictured her—
thin and blond and a bit serious (the chair), but also a little
wild inside (the red-berried plant),
but kind of elegant, too (the hat).
It was a neat idea, painting someone without the person
being there.

Jamie's regular portraits are real good, too.
He painted *Draft Age* in 1965, but I swear the guy who
posed for it
looks just like Michael Stitt.
He has Michael's attitude, too—chin up, head tilted to one side—
like he's sizing you up behind those dark lenses.
He'd fit right in with those guys
who hang out in the parking lot after school,
smoking cigarettes and acting cool.

There was another one of a man
with a pumpkin on his head (weird, but also interesting),
and the little sign said: "Pumpkin Head, Self-Portrait."
It's good to know that even
serious artists aren't completely humorless.

Jamie's portrait *Jeremy* reminded me a little of
Daddy. He had thick
blond hair and full lips—very handsome—
but in a quiet, pouty sort of way.

Jamie's people are good, but his animals are
even better. He does ducks, ravens, chickens, crows,
woolly sheep, and Black Angus cows.
He has a special fondness, though, for pigs.
He's painted them doing all sorts of things
that people do: pigs bathing and sleeping, pigs making friends
and staring out of windows, and even one trotting
beside a train. For his most famous pig painting,
he had a live model named Den-Den
who was so big, her portrait takes up one whole wall.
Imagine, Momma—
a life-size pink pig with fourteen teats and four small split
feet and fuzzy ears as large as visors.

I overheard a guide telling her tour group all about it:
"Jamie Wyeth fed Den-Den molasses and oats
to keep her still, and he played classical music
to keep her calm."

I never thought of pigs as particularly pretty, but
Den-Den is one beautiful hog. When you walk into that room,
you just have to look at her.

I want to paint like that someday.

In the meantime, I'm trying
to learn all I can from these Wyeth guys—
I am trying not to compare my plain little pencil sketches
or my charcoal drawings to their
gorgeous framed paintings (but it's hard).

19

When we first moved here from the trailer park,
our landlord, Mr. Kesey, used to invite me over after work
to sit on the porch (he has one of those big wicker swings).
Sometimes I'd bring him my school papers and my
drawings. He would look at them and ask me questions
about my teacher or the kids in my class.
He made me feel special and good, like I imagine
a grandfather would,
and once in a while I'd pretend
he *was* my grandfather.
On warm days we sat in that swing,
watching the horse graze
and sipping the lemonade he poured for us
into plastic cups.

According to Mr. Fitz, Mr. Kesey was married once,
a long time ago, but then he got divorced
and has lived alone ever since. I think he'd have made
a good father, but it doesn't seem like he'll ever
be one. Mr. Kesey runs a trucking business (the farm was
his father's—he keeps it as an investment, Daddy says),
and in the last few years he's gotten so busy
we hardly see him.

Yesterday on the shuttle bus, the driver was
sipping from a plastic cup, and I got to remembering

how Mr. Kesey was always nice to me, and how
he used to ask to see my drawings
and my schoolwork—and I wondered
if maybe *he* might be
anonymous.

20.

I tried to sketch Ella in her stall.
But every time she saw me, she came over to
nuzzle my pockets for treats. I spent all today
trying to find a way to keep her still.
I figure if Jamie Wyeth can call his painting *Portrait of Pig,*
then I can call my drawing
Portrait of Horse.

But you can't keep feeding a horse like you can
a pig. Horses don't know when to stop.
If they eat too much, their intestines get all twisted up
and they can die.

I tried music. We don't own any classical stuff,
so I played some of Daddy's old Springsteen tapes,
but they just made Ella nervous.

Momma, you know I can be really patient when I *want* to be . . .
but that darn horse almost out-stubborned me.
By four o'clock, I'd pretty much given up.
That's when Daddy sent me to the convenience store for more
milk and bread, and at the checkout they had
a stack of those disposable cameras—
twenty-four exposures for only $7.99.
Mr. Fitz had just paid me for last week's grooming,
so I bought one.

Back home, I dropped off the food and ran to the barn, where I
took twenty-four photos of

Ella standing,

       Ella chewing,

Ella rubbing her neck,

       Ella pawing,

Ella doing her laughing trick,

and I'm hoping a few will come out
good enough to sketch from.

I've noticed—
from reading those little white signs at the museum—
that a big part of making art
comes from being patient. When a Wyeth decides
he really wants to paint something,
he paints it, no matter what.
For example . . . when Andrew was young, he sketched nothing
but skeletons for months, to teach himself anatomy.
And once, he sketched his neighbor's house
in the midnight moonlight, then ran
back to his studio to make a painting from it (he finished
at four in the morning). Jamie sometimes paints

from inside a cardboard box so he doesn't get distracted,
and once *he* spent six months in a New York morgue
studying dead bodies
(personally, I'd prefer the skeleton method).

So I didn't give up either. I think I can make
a pretty decent drawing of Ella,
once those photos come back. I might not have a lot of talent,
but waiting is something I do
naturally.

21.

Every August, Daddy fills out these long blue forms
so I can get vouchers
for free food at school. Even so, I usually pack my own.
This morning, though, I was late. I grabbed one of the slips
from the cupboard and sprinted to catch the bus.

At lunch, I stood in line with the other
three hundred kids who buy, including Amanda Ray.
She rides my bus and lives five houses down from Tiffany,
and is just about the snobbiest (and therefore most popular)
girl in the whole school. Anyway,
she was behind me, loading her tray
with side dishes, desserts, and fruit, which she gives away
to Eddie Kuhnz and his table of most-popular guys.

She's flashing her twenty-dollar bill, and I'm taking
a bowl of chili and a slice of apple pie
and trying to hide my voucher, and Amanda says:
"Jeez, I thought a hardworking farm girl would eat more than that."

I felt like saying: "No, she really doesn't, and she doesn't
have to feed people like chickens to win friends, either,"
but I just shrugged and watched her chin rise a little higher
when the cashier took my voucher.

I sat at the last table with Danita and Marianne.
Right when I was finishing my pie, Amanda sauntered by

in her expensive jeans and sweater, and said:
"Hey, farm girl—I got an extra cookie, you want it?"
And I said, no, thanks, I'd had plenty, and she sneered
and threw it away. Marianne heard and called Amanda
a few things I won't repeat here.
Michael heard, too, and tripped Amanda
on the way back to class.

In math, I thought about all the things I want to say
but can't ever seem to say
to people like Amanda Ray who practice meanness
like it's a varsity sport.
Tiffany, on the other hand, would never hesitate
to say exactly what she felt at that moment,
to Amanda, or to anyone else in seventh grade.
I started to get a stomachache, but then I decided—
hey, later today, I'll just take Blake
for a little walk over to Amanda's house
and let him leave
a little brown gift on her lawn.

22

Daddy's truck is so old,
the bed has rusted through in places
and he has to keep patching it with pieces of metal
like a pair of hand-me-down jeans.

But it still *looks* pretty good. Mr. Kesey has a friend
with an auto-body shop, and he told Daddy
he would give him a price break on a new paint job
and even add a detail or two.
Daddy took it there and had it painted red
(it took three coats, he said, to cover the navy blue)
and had them put a white stripe
down each side and over the back fender.

Daddy was in a good mood
while he was cleaning it this morning,
so I asked him if he remembered the three of us
taking the truck up to Dennig's Corner
to watch the July 4th fireworks
when I was little. He kept rubbing the calf cloth harder
over the fender and bumper.
"Yes, of course I do."

He didn't look mad or sad, so I asked
if we could go back up there
and watch the fireworks again this year.
"Okay . . . yeah . . . maybe," he said.

He went on buffing and scrubbing for a while, not saying anything.
Then he grabbed that football—the one he takes
to throw with the construction guys on lunch breaks—
from the backseat, and threw it to me.

"Your momma was a true Southern lady," he told me
as we tossed it back and forth, "always mannerly and polite,
and she always kept her clothes and hair real nice. But she had
a throwing arm like a rocket, and me and her,
when we couldn't afford a movie or a restaurant for a date,
we'd go to a park in Savannah
and have a catch."

I tried not to look
surprised. But, Momma, I can count on one hand
the times since you died
that he has said *anything* about you.

The last time, it was Christmas, and I guess
I should've known better than to ask.
We were watching the original black-and-white TV version
of *Scrooge*, the one where I nearly wet my pants
when Marley's ghost comes stumbling in,
moaning and rattling his chains.
"Daddy, what did you and Momma do for Christmas
that first year you were together in Savannah?"

Daddy'd had two drinks (don't worry—he's still
not the drinking kind, but on holidays he likes a little wine),

so he told me:
"Your momma and me, we walked out into the woods
with a sack full of fabric scraps left over from her collages,
and we decorated the finest pine tree we could find
and smeared peanut butter on pinecones for the birds
and hung cranberries and popcorn strings
and then camped out for the night
(I guess it didn't get real cold in Georgia)
and in the morning we woke up to a chorus
of sparrows and finches and jays
feasting and chirping away."

But after he told me that, Daddy had to go
outside for about an hour,
and by the time he came back in, it was past 10:00,
and from his red-eyed look,
I promised myself that I would wait a long while until
the next time I made him
remember you.

23.

In art class, Miss Benedetto pulled me
aside and said she'd give me a pass to my next class
if I'd stay after.

When everyone had gone,
we sat down at one of the long painting tables,
and Miss B. asked me if I knew
what a grant was.
I said: "He's that general who fought at Gettysburg."
(Why can't I remember that in history class?)

She grinned and said I was right,
but there was another kind, too.
"The state gives money," she explained,
"to certain schools in certain years, for certain special programs,
and next year our district's getting one
for the arts."

I didn't know how this had anything
to do with me, but I listened on,
'cause I like Miss B.

"The grant—that's the money from the state—
is mostly for high school kids, but a few
middle school students can apply
with their teacher's approval.

Mrs. Davidson, the band leader, and I
would like you and Allison Larabee
(she's in eighth grade and plays classical guitar)
to give it a try."

She showed me the notice from the state
that explained everything. The students don't get money, exactly,
but if we get picked, we get to miss regular school
once a month or so
to go on special tours and trips
to places that will "foster our talents and creative instincts."
Miss B. said that meant museums and historic places, musical
concerts, ballets, and plays.

"Why me?" I asked.

And she said: "I think you're smart. I think
you are serious about art, and I think you have talent.
This might be helpful for your future."

I told her she was right about the *serious* part, but I
wasn't too sure about the *smart*. And I *wanted* to tell her
that I wasn't sure what Daddy would say, whether he would even
want me doing this.
I wanted to tell her about my visits
to the Brandywine River Museum, and that sometimes it felt like
I'd explode with all the questions I had about drawing
and about the paintings I'd seen. I wanted her to know

that sometimes living with Daddy's sadness,
and a hyper hunting dog,
and the ghost of my mother,
and a super-athletic best friend
was just too much.

I'm sure my face was red, and I could
feel the sweat trickling down the back of my neck.
My hands shook,
but I took the forms from Miss B.
and told her I'd fill them out
and bring them back by Friday.

Momma, we were not too religious
when you were here,
and we are not religious now. But if I believed in
guardian angels, Miss Joanna Benedetto
would be mine.

24.

I brought those forms back
to art class. I felt a little bad that I had to
trick Daddy into signing them—but not *too* bad. It wasn't
that hard. I just shuffled them in with a bunch of
other forms that parents have to sign, like

    rules for using the Internet in the library,
    the new traffic pattern for after-school carpools,
    permission to strike matches in science lab.

When he came to the grant application, I said—
as casual as I could—"This one's for a special sort of field trip"
(which isn't really a lie),
"here's where you need to sign,"
and he scribbled his name right on the dotted line.

Today, Miss B. sat down with me
to be sure I understood what to send the judges
(a panel of ten, according to the forms) so they can decide
who gets to be in the program
and who doesn't.

I asked Miss. B. if she thought, for the "portfolio" part,
I should do all five of the
required "samples of the student's best work"
in charcoal, pencil, or pen-and-ink.

"Use whatever you want, whatever makes you feel
most confident."

She flipped over the calendar on her desk,
and we counted a little more than four weeks
till those five samples are due in April. She gave me some
colored pencils and sketch pads, two boxes of charcoal,
and a can of fixative to spray on the best ones
so they don't smudge.

Next, from the bottom drawer of her desk,
she pulled out a rabbit's foot key chain.
"For good luck—you can give it back
when the judging's done."

I didn't know she was superstitious, but I guess
she is. Anyway, I can use all the help I can get
to compete with those high schoolers,
who probably know a lot more about drawing
and probably have a lot more
talent and experience than I do. Momma,
if anything about art is inherited,
now would be a very good time
for your genes to kick in.

25.

Why would you put a wild animal
on a door? I'm not sure, but that's exactly what
Jamie Wyeth did for one of his paintings.
The door (off its hinges, flat on the floor)
is smooth and white,
and the animal's resting there, like maybe he's
tired after breaking it down.

Jamie's wolf is not from a cartoon or a fairy tale—
this wolf looks real. He has a thin body, small eyes, and his expression
is shifty. Jamie made his fur red, and he layered the paint
to make it look all ruffled up
(if you push your ear against the wall where it's hanging,
like I did when the guard wasn't looking,
you can see the paint piled on the canvas like one of those
3-D geography maps), and if you stand there long enough, staring,
you have to stop yourself
from patting him.

On the bus ride back,
I thought about what subjects I sketch best.
I guess I would have to say
animals, 'cause I'm around them almost as much
as people.

At home, Daddy left a message
saying he was stuck in traffic on the turnpike
and I should go ahead and eat.

The days are longer and warmer now and there's still plenty
of good light . . . so after Blake and I each had a bowl
of Cheerios, I took him out and made him lie down
on an old stall door I've seen leaning against the barn.
He whimpered awhile, but I made him mind,
and I sketched him three different times.

It didn't work.
He looked so uncomfortable lying there—
his face, usually handsome, looked all worried and twisted,
and his back was stiffened up.
My three sketches stunk.

I quit and took him for a run instead.
He found his favorite gopher den again,
and I let him sniff it as long as he wanted. I could tell
that the gopher wasn't far down,
'cause Blake's tail wagged as fast as a windshield wiper.
          Poor little gopher, I thought. *Must be scared . . .*

Then my mind wandered like it always does. . . .
          What did Blake's pointy spaniel face
          look like from inside that dark place?
And for a few minutes, it was like I *became* that gopher.
My hand started working on a new drawing,
and before I knew it, without hardly trying,
I had a sketch that just might be
the best one I've ever done.

26.

This evening, Channel 6 News played a rerun tape
of the day Punxsutawney Phil
was supposed to see his shadow.

He climbed out of his den, all right, but there were so many
TV cameras and microphones,
he took one look at those reporters
and ducked back in.

I have days like that ... when I want to pull up the covers
and make the world go away,
pretend no one will notice if I stay home. But I have no
good reason to miss school—
I hardly ever get sick, and when I do, Daddy insists
on coming home from work.
(I'm sure it reminds him of losing you
to that one-week pneumonia—
but how could he know you were that sick?
And by the time you let him get a doctor, you were
too weak to walk, and nothing they gave you worked.)

Last winter, I had a bad flu.
Daddy stayed by my bed and fed me
noodle soup and toast and tea. The foreman got mad
and said Daddy had to get a sitter and get himself back to work
or he'd be fired.

Daddy thought about it overnight. The next morning,
he quit. That afternoon, the foreman called again
and said Daddy could have off for my flu,
but he shouldn't tell anyone on his crew.
I got better two days later.
Daddy went back to work. I went back to school.
But I still can't eat noodle soup without picturing Daddy
wearing his construction apron, standing over our little stove,
stirring the pot with his big tan hands,
and Blake whining and pacing and licking my face,
and all of us wishing
you were here.

27.

I haven't told Daddy yet—about the museum, I mean.
There hasn't been a right time. He's so beat
when he gets home. And besides,

if he knew I was visiting an art museum,
just like you probably did
when you lived in Savannah, well . . .
that might make him mad—or maybe sad—or maybe both.

The truth is, I haven't told Daddy yet because
I'm scared of what he might do.
What if he says I can't go there anymore?

I wish whoever *anonymous* is
could talk to Daddy, could remind him
there are *lots* worse things
I could be doing with my time.

You know, even if I told him, and even if he said
I wasn't allowed to go there anymore, I'm pretty sure
I'd go there anyhow, just like I'm doing now.

So, I suppose him knowing
isn't going to change anything,
so why get him upset?

28.

But I *did* tell Tiffany. This morning on the bus,
she fell asleep again listening to her CDs. I had nothing to do,
so I sketched her as a pumpkin wearing headphones
and carrying a lacrosse stick.

When she woke up, she asked: "What's the pumpkin for?"
so I told her about seeing Jamie Wyeth's self-portrait
at the museum, and how I was trying to learn
by copying his idea.

Of course, being Tiffany, she wanted to know
how long I'd been visiting,
and how often I go,
and how do I get there,
and does my daddy know,
and sometime if one of her practices gets canceled,
could she come with me?

I made her promise not to tell.
She swore on her new pair of cleats that she wouldn't
(especially Daddy).
I told her that guests were allowed anytime, and since I was
an official member, I would consider taking her
if she thought she could dress appropriately
and pay for her entry.

I was kidding, of course, about the clothes
(you can wear anything you like) and the money
(only five dollars for a student, which I *know* she can afford),
but seeing as how Tiffany
probably won't have a free afternoon anytime soon,
none of that really matters.

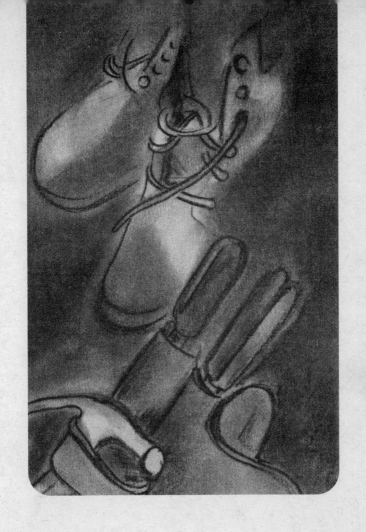

part 3

"It's the hardest work in the world to try

not to work!"

—N. C. Wyeth

29.

Marianne Ferlinghetti invited me
        to her thirteenth-birthday party
            at the Bowling Palace.

This morning on the bus, she gave me
        an invitation she'd made herself
            that had a drawing of a cake

sitting on a table, with yellow frosting
        and blue roses, and gifts of all
            shapes and sizes floating over it.

Tiffany didn't say anything, but I
        know what she was thinking.
            She and her friends call Marianne's

group of friends "the potheads"—
        and for the most part, they are right.
            Which is why—even though Marianne and I

have known each other since kindergarten
        and her mother brought food
            to Daddy and me after you died—

I am careful not to spend too much
        time with Marianne's friends. They still ask me
            to hang out after school at the old shed

behind the Longwood Baptist Church.
　　　Some days, there's a part of me
　　　　　that wants to say yes. Maybe I am too

picky. Maybe they would let me hang out with them
　　　and not smoke (but I doubt it).
　　　　　I don't seem to fit in to a group—

the Jocks, the Brains, the Preps, the Goths—
　　　like most of the other seventh graders,
　　　　　but I'm not uptight about it.

Mrs. Yocum thinks I should make more
　　　of an effort—last year, she gave me this book
　　　　　called *Fitting In: Social Skills for Shy Kids*

that had cartoons of students who looked
　　　like aliens and sidebars with hints about
　　　　　"establishing trust" and "knowing your boundaries."

I looked through it one night and then
　　　threw it in the trash. My boundaries
　　　　　are pretty well set, and if I decide

to move them, I'll be sure to tell Mrs. Yocum.
　　　In the meantime, Blake and Ella and Tiffany
　　　　　are just about all I can handle.

30.

"Georgia, you have to come over
right now. It's awful, just awful. All of them
at once—oh, God. . . ."

That was Tiffany on the phone this afternoon. She was half-
crying (and Tiffany almost *never* cries)
and her voice sounded funny—almost shy and kind of whimpery
(Tiffany is *not* shy or whimpery).

I ran.
And the whole way over, I'm thinking
how weird she's been lately—too tired one day,
too jittery the next—
and I'm guessing what the "all of *them*" might be. . . .
Maybe she'd had enough and she just
up and quit all her sports at once,
or maybe her big shelf of trophies
(and there are a *lot* of them)
came crashing down on her head,
or maybe she knocked out all her teeth
with a lacrosse stick.

By the time I arrived, my stomach was in knots
and I was out of breath.
I found Tiffany in her room, standing over her fish tank,
her tears *plunk-plunking* into the water.

About a month ago, Tiffany decided she needed
a pet, but since she's hardly ever home,
she doesn't have time for a dog or even a cat,
and she doesn't like hamsters or gerbils or snakes.
I suggested fish.
"They're easy to take care of," I said.
"And they're really good for stress."

And being Tiffany, she didn't buy just one or two, she bought
twelve—just like a girl's lacrosse team. She even got one
with an exotic tail and named it Goalie.

But something went wrong with the water or with the filter,
'cause they were all belly-up in the tank,
some on the bottom, and some drifting slowly
on the current, like lost souls.
It was a sad sight. It was a lot less sad, though,
than the other things I'd been imagining,
so I sat on the edge of Tiffany's bed,
put my head between my knees,
and caught my breath.

When I looked up, Tiffany's tears had stopped, and those
twelve upside-down, slow-drifting fish looked so pathetic—
I couldn't help it—I started laughing.

I thought Tiffany would be mad, but then she laughed, too,
and soon we were both

rolling around on the floor,
clutching our sides.

Then Tiffany's brother, Teddy, came in (he's in fifth grade).
He said: "Hey, let me flush them for you,"
but Tiffany insisted on a proper burial for her "team."

Teddy helped us net them
and put them in a cookie tin. We took it outside and dug
a small hole under one of the scraggly twigs they call "trees"
in Tiffany's neighborhood.

After a moment of silence, I played "We Are the Champions"
on Teddy's portable CD player. Tiffany asked me
what she should say for the eulogy,
and when I said: "I don't know, I've never been to a funeral,"
she looked shocked.
"I guess you should say something nice about each one,
but since there were a dozen,
and they were small, maybe one thing about them all
would be enough."

We bowed our heads and Tiffany said
how they put up a good fight, how they all
stuck together in their tank and none of them
were selfish. Except she said "shellfish" and that made us
start laughing all over again. I said a final "Amen"
and we went inside to find something to eat. That's when

Tiffany asked me: "How come you didn't go
to your mother's funeral?"

So I told her: "The night Momma died, I cried and cried
and couldn't stop,
and I went into shock
and had to stay in the hospital.
Daddy had to go back and forth
between the funeral home and me, and while he was visiting,
Momma's folks took over."

I told her how, behind Daddy's back, they had you cremated
and took your ashes to Savannah,
so that's how come I never went to your funeral
or saw your grave, or, as Mrs. Yocum would say,
"had closure."

Tiffany's eyes opened real wide,
like they always do when I tell her something
she can hardly believe.
She asked her mother if she could skip practice
"just for tonight," and Mrs. O'Neill said:
"All right, but don't make it a habit."

We made a huge bowl of popcorn and watched a few
game shows on TV. Teddy needed help
with his science project
(he's growing seeds in gravel and tea leaves)

and then all three of us played one-handed War,
which we'd decided we liked more
than the two-handed version.

They both walked me home. On the hill,
we picked a bunch of early violets and wild daffodils.
Tiffany chattered constantly
about nothing in particular, the way only Tiffany can do,
and I realized this must be the first time—in a long time—
that she didn't have to be on a field or in a gym,
or in front of the Sisters, reciting scripture.

At the pasture, Mr. Fitz was turning Ella loose
after training her. The three of us leaned on the gate
and watched Ella race across the field, bucking and whinnying,
so relieved to be free.

31.

It was seventy-nine degrees today—
warmer than usual for April—
and a perfect day to sketch. But that's not
what I did. Instead, I spent the better part of the afternoon
trying to find Miss Benedetto's lucky rabbit's foot.
I lost it when I ran over to Tiffany's, so it's definitely
somewhere out there
in those five acres of fields
between our trailer and her neighborhood.

As I was looking, I couldn't help thinking
that this was one of those times, if I had a grandmother—
the kind that bundles you up in the cold
and makes you chocolate chip cookies
and lets you watch anything you want on TV—
this would be exactly the kind of time
a grandmother like that
would help me. She'd put on her flat-
soled shoes and her grandmother sweater,
and she'd walk the fields with me, searching.
Or she might offer to drive me somewhere
to buy a new rabbit's foot
to replace the one I lost (even though I didn't mean to).

But I don't know my grandmother. I have
no one like that to call.

Instead, I need some other kind of good luck charm
to help me find the one I lost. . . . But mostly
I need the guts to tell Miss Benedetto
that I have been careless
with her gift.

32.

Every night for the past week,
I've been trying to sketch Daddy. After dinner, he stretches out
on the couch to watch TV, and he's usually
fast asleep by 8:30. That's when I
grab my sketch pad and sit at his feet, but every drawing
I've made so far—for some reason—
just isn't working.

Then yesterday at the museum,
I found Andrew Wyeth's *Trodden Weed*.
The sign said "Tempera," and that Andrew had
mixed powdered pigment with egg yolk
and had painted slowly and in layers,
to get in all the details. The painting is a man,
but you can only see him from the knees down. He wears
a loose black coat and leather boots, and he's stepping
on a big weed.

The sign also said it was
Andrew's self-portrait, which he painted
after he'd been really sick. I guess the weed he's trampling
is Death, and he's showing how he beat it.

Right after that, I walked back to look at
Jamie Wyeth's portrait of his wife—
the one with the plant, the chair, and the hat—

and that made me think about *things* . . .
how they can tell you a lot
about a person, how each object
is a story.

I got home early enough to fix us a hot
chicken dinner. While we were eating, Daddy asked:
"You been keepin' yourself busy around here after school?"

I nodded and tried not to
choke on my chicken wing.
"Yep," I said. "With the horses and homework and . . ."

Daddy chewed and waited for me to finish.
I should have said "watching TV" or "playing with Blake,"
but instead all I said was ". . . and other stuff."

Daddy shoveled in his last bite.
He looked like he wanted to say something, but then
he closed back up again.

That was it—that was all we said.
He helped me clear the table and went off
to watch sports.

I was washing the dishes when I noticed
Daddy's work boots and his tool belt
leaning against each other near the door, like two old friends.

Above them, through the glass, was Mr. Kesey's willow tree,
which is as huge and droopy
as the magnolias I've seen in pictures of Savannah,
like the one you were sitting under
the day you met Daddy.

So while Daddy's eyes were glued to Channel 10,
I grabbed my drawing pad and my best ink pen
and started his portrait.

33.

Today was Marianne's birthday party
at the Bowling Palace. I didn't go.
Two weeks ago, Mr. Fitz asked me if I could spend today
getting Ella bathed, groomed, and braided
for the Unionville Horse Show.
I said yes and I guess that was lucky,
'cause I didn't really want to go to that party
but I didn't want to lie
to get out of it.

I had just finished bathing Ella
and was walking her along the lane so she'd dry in the sun,
when Tiffany came flying up the hill.
She started jabbering away about her uncle Ray
who'd come to visit from Florida.
She was in a hyper mood, but she seemed happy enough,
and I could tell she liked having him around.
"He tells me stuff about my mother when she was younger,"
Tiffany told me. Then she asked: "So, G. . . . If you don't know
your grandparents,
and you have never met your great-uncle Doug,
then how do you know all that stuff
about your mother?" So I explained.

"Just before Momma got sick, it was
Christmastime. She must have been thinking about

the past, about Savannah." *(Do you remember that, Momma?)*
"She showed me a photograph of her brother,
and another one of herself with her mother
and father. But it was after her brother had died,
and their smiles looked fake, like they were painted on.
I remember she looked—already—like a dog chained too tight,
like she was desperate to escape."

The rest of it, I told Tiffany, I got from Daddy
over the last six years—but only in little bits, now and then,
here and there. I have learned to watch him, like you might watch
a slow leak from a faucet. Sometimes it takes forever
before you see a single drip,
and if you time it right, you can catch it in your hand,
but you gotta be *quick*.

"Do you still have the photographs—
of your mother's brother? And your grandparents?"

"I'm pretty sure Daddy tore them up," I said.
"He might've even burned them. . . ."

Just then, Daddy drove up the lane in his truck.
He stopped beside us, said he had to
get some supplies from the lumberyard for Mr. Kesey,
and could I come along for a few minutes to help?
That was good—I didn't have to tell Tiffany about that week
before we moved our trailer out of the park,

when I rode with Daddy three times to this place in the woods,
where he made a big fire
and dumped boxes full of your stuff
into the flames.

I remember standing next to him,
wondering if that was what hell looked like
and praying
you weren't there.

34.

"Paints, Paper, and Clay—Artwork by the Students
of Longwood High, Grades 9–12."

That's what the sign said at the bottom of
the big glass showcase next to the nurse's office.
I was on my way there for some of those
fruit-flavored Rolaids (I didn't do so hot
on Mr. Krasinski's exponents test),
but once I noticed that exhibit,
I spent the next class period looking at:

> miniature landscape paintings,
> cut-paper collages,
> metal sculptures,
> watercolors,
> pen-and-ink portraits,
> ceramic vases and plates.

To me, every piece
looked perfect—every one of those high schoolers
knew what they were doing.

After gym class, I got a pass and found
Miss Benedetto. I told her I wanted to
withdraw my application for the grant program,
the sooner the better.

"I've seen what I'm up against," I told her,
"and I don't stand a chance."

Miss B. pulled together two chairs, and we sat there
in silence for a while. "Georgia," she said at last,
"I've seen some pretty incredible sketches
on the covers of your math book, not to mention
the stuff you've done in class.
I would not have you do this if I didn't think your work
was at *least* as good as theirs.
Of course, I'm not one of the judges,
so there's no guarantee. . . .
But how will you know what you can do
unless you try?"

I started to argue, and for once the words felt like
they would actually come out, but she said:
"Trust me—you just hand in your five best pieces
and let the judges decide."
I promised her I'd finish my portfolio.
I promised her I'd try.

But I didn't tell her I'd lost her rabbit's foot—the one
I was counting on
to get me in.

35.

I saw Tiffany talking to Ronnie Kline
in the hall, before first period.
Tiffany has hardly even *looked* at Ronnie Kline before,
and now she is talking to him???!!! Hmmmmmm . . .
Ronnie I-always-smell-like-cigarettes Kline,
whose older brother got arrested last year
for selling drugs at the high school,
is *not* the kind of guy who has casual conversations
with well-dressed popular athletes
like Tiffany O'Neill.

So today after math, I asked Tiffany why
she was talking to Ronnie Kline.
"He just wanted to know who won the game yesterday."
Then she looked away quick.

Momma, I know you never met Tiffany,
but I know Tiffany better than
just about anyone else—
sometimes even herself—
and I can tell you, Tiffany O'Neill may be a lot of things—

like reckless,
like pouty,
like funny,
like even snobby sometimes. . . .

But until today, Tiffany has not been
a liar.

36

It takes a lot of people to make a house. I never knew
how many until Daddy took me
to work. I can't say why he did, exactly,
except I guess he felt guilty leaving me alone
on my two days off (our teachers have an "in-service"—
Miss Benedetto says that's when they take
classes to help them teach better, but since the lectures
are mostly for teachers of English or math,
she draws caricatures of the speakers).

Or maybe Daddy knows I'm not
staying home all the time when he's at work
and he wants to keep me away from
the kids who spend their free time
smoking or drinking or stealing, the kids who
really *belong* on that "At Risk" list.

Anyway, today I ended up in his truck, bleary-eyed
at 5:30 in the morning, heading west
to Lancaster County, where I spent the day
watching him and about ten other men
slap up drywall and frame out windows and doors,
fit crossbeams, and nail down the floor. A few others
came and went, pouring cement and fitting gutters
on the roof (you couldn't pay me enough to do that—
they have to walk back and forth across the house

about fifty feet up,
sure-footed as mountain goats but loaded down
with tools and nails
and no telling when there'll be a breeze).

After lunch, Daddy took out his football, and the masons played
the carpenters in two-hand touch.
But one of the carpenters had a bad knee, so Daddy yelled over
to where I was sitting under the one scraggly tree:
"Hey, Georgia, c'mon!"

Well, Momma, these guys are all about six feet tall,
and they pound nails and lift boards eight hours a day.
Then there's me—five-foot-one, and while I'm strong for my size
from handling horses and doing chores,
I am no linebacker, either.

I gave Daddy a sideways look that told him
I didn't think this was one of his better ideas.
But he just clapped his hands together and said:
"You can be the QB, and we'll do all the runnin'."

So there I was, Momma—me and the carpenters and masons
playing touch football in the middle of some former cornfield
way out in Lancaster County.

The window guys sat in their trucks and cheered
while I threw a dozen pretty good passes—
only one bad one, short and out-of-bounds—

and Benny caught three for touchdowns
and Daddy caught one,
and the rest got us enough good yardage
to win 35 to 10.

Benny and Sal carried me
on their shoulders to the truck, where we
shared iced tea and a package of Oreos.
They lit cigarettes, strapped on their tools,
and went back to work.

But Daddy didn't.
He stood next to me for the longest time,
not saying anything. I figured he was thinking about you,
about the past, but this time,
he didn't look sad.

"You throw real good," he finally said. "Your momma'd
be proud." Then he pointed to the house. "You ever wish
we lived in one like this?"

I shrugged. "Sometimes. Once in a while . . . it'd be nice,
I guess, to have an oven you could put a whole pizza in,
and a closet with a door and light. Other than that,
it'd be way too big for you and me,
and it'd be a real pain to clean."

And Momma, Daddy laughed. He *laughed*.

37.

Went to Lancaster again. I asked Daddy
if he thought it'd be all right to sketch a few of the workers.
I told him I had a project to do for art class
(which isn't a real lie; my portfolio *is* a project and it *is* for art).
He said: "Better ask them first."

When we got there, Benny and Sal
were unloading a flatbed full of wood and they both said:
"Sure, you can sketch me as long as I can keep my clothes on."
(Wise guys, both of them.) I found two cement blocks to sit on,
propped them in a corner, and watched them get to work.

It's funny how, when you look at someone for a long time,
you start to notice certain things.
For example, without his baseball cap,
Benny's hair puffs up wilder than Einstein's
(Mrs. Bigelow has a poster of him in the science room),
and he has long, flexible fingers like a pianist.
He leans over a piece of wood like it's a baby,
and lifts it like it's a baby,
and turns it this way and that, like it's gonna
speak to him at any moment.
Sal, on the other hand, is built like a bull and moves
around the house like it's *his* house and the wood had better
do exactly what he wants.
He has short, stubby fingers, and big shoulders and legs,

and his Marlboro sticks out of his mouth,
wiggling like a snake.

I sketched them both—three times—and they were
real cool about it. I think they even liked it.
Then I made another quick sketch of the window framer,
and one of the stonemason, who has
the loneliest eyes.

The framer called me "honey" and ruffled my hair like I was
a six-year-old, but the other guys were pretty nice and didn't
make me feel like I shouldn't be there, like I was
too young or too much
in the way.

No football today. It rained a little at lunch,
so the guys drove
to the 7-Eleven or stayed inside.

Before we left, Benny gave me an apron that said
"Figaro Bros. Carpenters and Woodworkers—since 1967."
He asked me if I was coming back, and I told him I go to
public school and we didn't have another break until May.

Then he asked if he could see
my sketchbook. I let him have it awhile, and he took his time.
He looked at each sketch, and on some of them
he took longer and made clucking noises with his tongue.

"You are so much like your mother," he said
when he handed it back to me.

The whole ride home I wondered
how many others knew you
better than I ever will.

38.

When we pulled in to school this morning,
Tiffany jumped up, grabbed her stuff, said "Bye,"
and got off the bus in a hurry.

I waited until the eighth graders passed,
then walked to my locker. Down the hall,
I saw Ronnie Kline hand something to Tiffany,
and she handed him
something back.

39

Two nights ago, Daddy opened the shoe box
he keeps on the shelf above his bed
and took out the little black address book
that I forgot he had.
We don't have much use for address lists. Since Daddy
grew up in the boys' home in Georgia
and has no family at all, we don't
even send Christmas cards.

On the front of that little book in big gold letters, it said:
"Tamara and David McCoy."
I wonder if Daddy gets that same fluttery feeling
inside—like I do—whenever he reads
your name.

Anyhow, Daddy needed the address of the auto parts supplier
so he could send for a filter
to replace the old one in his truck. But seeing that little black book
got me to thinking how easy it'd be
to look up your parents' address
and maybe even write them a letter.

The birthday cards from Great-Uncle Doug are nice,
but I think I'd really like to be in touch
more often
with your relatives. Even if we never meet,

I'd like to write to someone
with the same blood in their veins,
who maybe even has a nose like mine,
someone who has memories of you just like I do,
but who would actually *talk* about them . . .
someone who knew you when you were my age and could tell me
what you were like.

I couldn't sleep for thinking about it.
All night and most of the next day, I kept
imagining and planning everything I'd say—
I might write your parents a short letter first,
mail it in Delaware when we go shopping
(I'm sure I could slip it in the mailbox
outside the grocery store when Daddy wasn't looking).

I wouldn't tell Daddy, of course.
But I'd write to your folks and tell them
that I was alive and doing okay, and that I had
brown hair and blue eyes, just like you did,
and a habit of sketching and drawing, just like you,
and that you were a good mother,
and I missed you,
and maybe I'd even promise to come and visit them
in Savannah when I'm grown.

Since Mrs. Yocum started me
writing to you in this diary,

it's got me believing
it'd be fun to write to someone and actually have them
write back (no offense, Momma).

So I thought—maybe if this goes well, maybe if it
feels like a good thing to do—
I might work up the nerve to write to Great-Uncle Doug,
and I would ask him to write back,
even when it's not my birthday.

After school, I ran up the lane
and took that shoe box down
from Daddy's shelf.
My hands were shaking like they did
when Miss Benedetto showed me
those grant forms.

I opened it slowly and flipped
through all the pages.
Except for a few A entries for auto parts places,
and a few F's for Figaro Bros. Carpenters,
and Mr. Kesey in the K's, of course,
it was nearly empty.

When I flipped back to S, I saw
the space where your parents' address must have been. *Speare*.
It was scratched out hard with a black pen.
I held the page up to the window.

I turned it all around—this way and that way—
and I still could not make out
one single, solitary letter.

I put it down, feeling it with my fingertips,
trying to read it like someone who's blind. But whoever
scratched out that address
left nothing behind.

40.

Something's different about Tiffany.
She's keeping a secret. I think she should be
telling me what's going on—

After all, I have told her *my* secrets
(including some things about you). Isn't that
what good friends are supposed to do?

At least I could listen. She knows I wouldn't tell.
But whatever it is, she's not saying.
For the first time since we've been friends,

Tiffany is avoiding me. We don't talk like we
used to in the halls. She doesn't return my calls,
and we don't always sit together on the bus.

It's like she's drawn a curtain between us,
and even though I'm trying to see through it,
we're still on opposite sides.

41.

Only one week until
my portfolio is due. I am working on my drawings every
afternoon and almost every evening
after Daddy falls asleep.

Miss Benedetto gave me a big cardboard folder
to keep my drawings in,
which just fits inside my closet.
I forgot, though, that Blake likes to lie down in there
(he's not allowed on my bed),
and one night he plopped right on top of it
and bent the edges of my best pencil sketch.

I rolled it out on my bed, put my schoolbooks
on either end, and slept on the floor with Blake.
By morning, it looked pretty good again—just a little crease—
so I'm planning to hand it in. I told Blake to find another place
to lie down or I'd have to tie him outside
(his new spot is the heat vent—on cool nights, I have to
wear a sweater, but at least my drawings are safe).

Did you know that Andrew Wyeth painted
this lady named Helga—sometimes she's inside posing nude,
and other times she's standing outside by a tree,
wearing a big green cape and braids?
For fourteen years he didn't tell anyone, *even his wife*.

He hid two hundred pictures of her
in his neighbor's house, and when they were discovered,
Helga made all of the papers,
and the cover of *Time*.

Andrew was lucky to have that hiding place.
My closet barely holds my clothes and shoes,
let alone my portfolio (I'm saving every sketch
until I decide which five are the best),
which gets thicker all the time.

Besides, I am just drawing innocent farm animals,
some construction guys, and a few still lifes.
But if I happen to meet a handsome man wearing a cape
and leaning against a tree,
I believe Andrew Wyeth himself would be disappointed
if I didn't ask him to pose.

42

Big puddle on the floor this morning,
but luckily it was
nowhere near my drawings.

When we got back from food shopping,
Daddy took me with him to Lancaster,
where he bought the supplies he needed at a wholesaler
to fix our leaky roof.

He also picked up his overtime check,
which put him in a real good mood. Daddy is still
what you'd call a direct driver, a no-stopping-for-anything
kind of man. But when I asked: "Can we stop, real quick,
at one of those Amish farm stands?"
he said sure.

We bought cheese and jam and homemade muffins
that smelled so good, we each ate two. We got stuck
in traffic on Lancaster Pike,
and that's when I saw—in one Amish farmer's field—
the billboard ad for Six Flags park.
It was a close-up photo of people on the
downturn of a roller coaster, with their hair
pinned back by wind and their mouths twisted.
I thought how it must be so weird for that Amish farmer,
with his long beard, his black hat, his suspenders and plain black suit,

to follow his mule team and his plow
under that roller coaster picture
every spring.

Momma, this is exactly the kind of thing
I would talk to you about
if you were here.
This is exactly the kind of thing that I would never tell
Tiffany. She doesn't think like that.
I would tell her, and she would laugh and say:
"Georgia, you are strange. Who cares
what some Amish guy thinks?"

Actually, there's a part of me that would like to be
more like Tiffany—someone who's too busy to think
too much. But another part of me believes
there must be a *reason* that some of us notice,
that some of us wonder,
why Amish guys should have to plow
beneath roller coaster billboards.

"Artists notice things that other people don't.
They're very observant," Miss B. told our class the other day.
Michael Stitt said: "Isn't that just another way
of saying they're weird?" . . . which Miss B. ignored.
(But he might be right.)

I guess if you're an artist, you have to learn
to keep your mouth shut around people who don't see things

the way you do.
Well, keeping my mouth shut has never been hard.
It would just be nice, once in a while, to tell somebody
something curious like that
and have them understand.

43.

Sometimes when I try, I can look at Daddy
like he's any other guy, not like he's
my father, and I can see why
you fell for him.

Like on Saturday . . . The checkout lady at the Acme in Delaware
starting flirting with him right in front of me!
I could tell Daddy was annoyed, but that didn't
stop her. I glared when she sent me to produce
to check the price of Idaho potatoes.
When I walked back toward our line, I saw
a tall, tanned man with strong arms
and soft gray eyes—a big shyness about him.

Momma, in case you're wondering, your husband is
still pretty handsome, but these days he's not
putting that fact to very much use.
Maybe he wouldn't be so sad if he had
a little female company.
But when that time comes, he'd better not choose
that batty-eyed, smooth-talking, air-brained Acme lady.
No way. *Sad* is one thing . . . *desperate*
is another.

44.

After lunch, Tiffany came over to my table.
It's been a while since she's done that.
Close up, I could see her eyes had
dark circles (she was wearing makeup to try and hide them,
but I could still tell).

She asked about Blake, about Ella, about
my drawing. I asked about

lacrosse (the school team),
tournaments (with her club team),
swimming (her summer team's already practicing),
religious classes.

She said: "Good, all goin' good . . ."
like it was a tape she played
whenever someone asked.

Then she said *I* looked pretty tired,
and I told her I'd stayed up late
to finish a sketch.

"Here," she said, "try one,"
and offered me these yellow capsules—
"They help me keep awake. They work pretty good, too."

I looked around quick to see
if anyone was watching (they weren't).
I couldn't believe she would be so stupid.
It explained why she looked like
a zombie, though.

The bell rang and Jess Bettis, one of Tiffany's basketball friends,
came by to say hi, and then Michael Stitt
plowed into us as we were leaving, and I didn't have to
do anything about those pills. She slipped
them back into her pocket, and we all
walked our separate ways in the hall,
and for the first time ever, I was actually *glad* to be
heading to history.

45.

Living History Day at school. Everyone in the whole
seventh grade had to dress up
like a famous person from the nineteenth century.
Last week, we picked names from a hat and I got
Annie Oakley. But I lost the handout Mr. Hendershot gave us
explaining how to get a good grade, so I
remembered as much as I could and guessed at the rest.
I remembered I needed a costume and I should look up stuff
about my person and give a short report
(I forgot the time line and bibliography parts).

Tiffany loaned me her brother's old
holsters and toy pistols—they're plastic, but even so,
our principal, Mr. Nardo, had to inspect them in homeroom—
and Mr. Fitz let me borrow his Western hat, a pair of chaps,
and his daughter's snakeskin boots
in exchange for two hours of grooming.

Michael Stitt and Adam McVey spent half the day
slipping the pistols from my holsters and the other half
knocking off my hat.
"Michael likes you," Marianne whispered in math.

Michael Stitt? He *is* kind of cute . . .
and he's smart . . . and I think he does like art class
(but he won't admit it).

But I can think of better ways
to get my attention than stealing my guns
and plowing into me at lunch. Maybe
I could sketch him. . . .

Anyway, it was Living History Day, and I don't like
history much—too many wars and acts and treaties—
but I *did* kind of like Annie Oakley. Did you know
that her father died when she was five,
and she started hunting (with a real gun)
to feed her mother and her brothers and sisters?
Annie got so good at shooting that she started
selling furs to traders
and made enough money to go to the city
and join a Wild West show. She married the owner,
and the two of them traveled all over the country, even
to London so Annie could sharpshoot for the queen.

"Well done!" Mr. Hendershot said after my presentation.
I got points off for "lack of eye contact"
(I get too nervous if I look at the class,
so I stare down at my notes),
but he gave me five extra points for "superior details"
and one more for "putting up with difficult props."

We did a play for the parents,
and even some aunts and uncles came. Afterward, I felt
worn-out, and my stomach started to hurt, so I
got a pass to the nurse.

Mrs. Reed was expecting me (this always happens
when the parents are invited—I know Daddy can't
afford to give up a day's pay, but it'd be nice if someday
he came, too, like the other parents do).
She had my fruit-flavored Rolaids all ready
and cleared the papers off the couch
and set the goldfish bowl right where I could see it.
"Stay as long as you want," she said.

I lay down and thought about Daddy
pounding nails somewhere
and Tiffany looking like a zombie, trying to give me pills
that remind me of the kind I've seen Mrs. Reed
give to kids who have a special prescription for them,
to help them concentrate. I tried not to worry about it.
I tried to watch the fish.

Meanwhile, Mrs. Reed went back to her desk
to fill out a form for who visits the nurse,
how often, and why,
that she probably has to send to Guidance,
which probably keeps me
on that stupid "At Risk" list.

46

Miss B. showed us slides of paintings by
Vincent van Gogh and Paul Gauguin.
Most of us had seen Van Gogh's *Starry Night* and those
famous purple irises. They put them on
calendars and mouse pads and even on T-shirts
you can buy in Wal-Mart.

But I've never seen Gauguin's stuff before.
"He was a successful businessman in Paris," Miss B. told us.
"But he also loved to paint. He had a midlife crisis,
left his wife and five kids, and sailed all the way
to Tahiti to live like a primitive."
(She glanced at Michael when she said that.)

Lots of beach scenes with coconuts, palm trees,
and canoes. Half-dressed women with long black hair
and brown skin. (Miss B. kept one hand on Michael's shoulder
as she flipped through the slides. He shut up this time.)
I liked the bright colors Gauguin used,
and the way you felt like you were in a dream.

Both men had their share of troubles, it seems.
Van Gogh sold only one painting his whole life.
He had seizures (he cut off his ear during one of them),
and later, he just got up from his easel and shot himself
in the middle of a field.

Gauguin had a rough time, too. He caught a bad sickness
called syphilis and died in Tahiti, penniless.

Michael asked why two such
talented guys ended up like that (a good question, I thought).
"Each artist is unique," Miss B. said. "They each lead
a different kind of life. Georgia O'Keeffe, for instance,
had lots of friends, lived to be ninety-eight,
and was pretty rich when she died. . . .
But artists are often way ahead of their time,
and it can be lonely when no one understands you."

I wondered if N. C. Wyeth studied Van Gogh
or Gauguin. He probably did. Maybe that's why
he encouraged all his kids to be creative—
he wanted one of them, at least one,
to understand.

47.

I must have looked tired again this morning
(I stayed up past midnight working on my drawings).
On the bus, Tiffany offered me two of those
yellow capsules, and when I said "No thanks,"
she took them both herself.

I know she's taking those
so she doesn't fall behind in school,
so she can play all her sports and finish CCD,
so she doesn't disappoint
her parents,
her coaches,
her teachers,
or the Sisters.

But how come I am the only one who notices
how bad she needs a rest?
And what kind of friend am I to stand by
and do nothing?

Anyway, my drawings are almost done. Tonight
I can do something fun, and tomorrow I'm sleeping late.
I asked Tiffany if she wanted to watch a movie with me,
but she has to play lacrosse
in a "select" tournament at Penn State.
She leaves right after school for the five-hour ride
and stays over for two nights.

When I said "Good luck," she just
stared through the window with a blank face
like she hadn't heard,
like she was watching a movie she'd seen
a hundred times.

48.

I'm getting a funny feeling, Momma.
Like that time last November when Daddy
had already left for work, but the roads were still
pretty icy and our school had a
two-hour delay. It was cold, all right, but it was sunny
and not too windy, and I had nothing to do,
so I took Blake for a walk.

After a few minutes or so, though,
I got this strange notion to run
home. I whistled to Blake to come back, and when
we got close to the trailer again,
he started barking like a maniac.

Inside, I saw why: Daddy had left the little space heater on,
and a stack of bills had fallen from the kitchen table
and landed right in front of it.
Little strings of smoke had started to rise, so I
yanked the cord out quick
and tossed the papers into the sink.
At dinner I told Daddy what happened.
"Good thing you turned back when you did," he said,
"or we'd be homeless."

Now I have that same funny feeling
whenever I'm with Tiffany—like I should run home

and put out some fire—but there is no fire,
just Tiffany acting okay sometimes but at other times
real tired and spaced out
or else super hyper—and Momma,

now I know why . . . but I
have no clue what to do.

49.

I've been looking at those pencil sketches I did
when I went to work with Daddy—the one of the stonemason
with the big, sad eyes, and the one of Benny with his
long arms and thin fingers. So far, they are
my best sketches of humans.

So . . . I'm going to touch up one and leave it in pencil,
and redo the second one in charcoal, and if they
come out all right, I'll spray the second one with fixative
so it doesn't smudge
and put them both in my portfolio.

What would those men say
if they knew
these drawings might someday
get me into college, or maybe art school?

Then again, when all this is done,
maybe I'll just have a nice bunch of drawings
that ten judges in Harrisburg will look at
and send back.

50.

Daddy left
early again this morning. Tiffany called to tell me
her father was taking her to school
'cause she had to bring her solar system project
and it would get wrecked on the bus,
and did I want a ride?

Perfect. I didn't know how I was going to get
my portfolio in to Miss B.
without getting it creased or smashed
on the bus, and now I didn't
have to worry.

I skipped homeroom, went straight to the art room,
and put the folder on Miss B.'s desk.
I was leaving when she walked in carrying
a chocolate doughnut. She offered me half and said:
"I'll give you a pass. Why don't you stick around
and show me what you have?"

We sat at one of the long painting tables
just like when we first talked about
the grant.
I pulled all five of my samples—
one by one—from the folder,
and laid them out.

Miss B. began at the left and moved slowly
toward the right, looking at them—one by one—
and then she came back to where she started
and did the very same thing all over again,
but this time she read the titles out loud:

"*Portrait of My Father,* still life, pen-and-ink.
Ella Laughing, animal portrait, charcoal.
Benny, human figure, charcoal.
The Stonemason, portrait, pencil.
Anybody Home?, animal portrait, pencil."

(That last one was Tiffany's idea. I didn't have
a good title for my picture of Blake's face
in the gopher hole, so I let her make one up.)
I couldn't tell what she was thinking
until she stopped chewing,
wiped her mouth with a napkin,
and said with a grin: "These are very, very good. . . .
But why do you look so sad?"

"I feel awful," I said. "I lost your rabbit's foot in our fields
while I was running my dog.
But I will buy you another, the same size and color,
at Wal-Mart the next time I get paid."

She pointed to her desk. "Open the drawer on the left."
Lined up inside, I counted
fourteen rabbit's feet—all sizes and colors.
"I don't need another," she said.
"And from what I see in this folder,
you don't either."

51.

After history, I saw Tiffany in the hall. She looked strange—
her eyes were dull and her
skin was real pale.
"Georgia, I don't feel so good," she said.
I said: "Go see Mrs. Reed. Lie down on her couch, watch the fish
until you can go home."

Mr. Hendershot yelled at us to get to class,
so I didn't see her after that.

I couldn't concentrate in science. I decided
to talk to Tiffany about those pills.
And if she wouldn't listen, and if she still
looked tired and sick, I'd tell someone—maybe Miss B.—
that she needed help.

But I never had to tell.

Tiffany didn't go see Mrs. Reed.
Instead, she went to gym class,
where they say she was jogging on the track when she
collapsed.

part 4

"[The idea] that I am recording something

nobody's looked at before, a unique view.

That's why I paint."

—Jamie Wyeth

52.

The school library says
I have two books overdue and would I
please return them soon
or pay $34.19
at the circulation desk.

I looked all over our trailer, and inside
Daddy's truck, and on the bus (every seat, twice),
and in all the pockets of my backpack,
and in every corner of my locker,
and at the front office lost and found,
and I still couldn't find them.

Then, right before lunch, when my
stomach was rumbling through Mr. Krasinski's lecture
on the distribution properties of improper fraction equations,
I suddenly remembered where I'd left them.

Mrs. Reed was busy cleaning up a sixth grader
with a bloody nose, so I stayed next to her desk
and waited. In one corner, I noticed a big stack of
those admitting forms, and on the other,
a notepad and two pens,
just like the ones I'd seen last week
at the little gift shop
in the lobby of the Brandywine River Museum.

Mrs. Reed had already set my library books aside:
The Life of Georgia O'Keeffe and *Savannah: A Visitor's Guide*.
"I thought they might be yours, but I wasn't sure."
Then she said: "Seems like I haven't seen you as much—
but I guess that's good, right?"

I wanted to ask her about that notepad and those pens,
about whether she was a member, or if
she had ever sponsored someone
anonymously,
but the kid's nose started flowing again,
so she ran back to help.

I picked up one of those museum pens, and wrote:

Dear Mrs. Reed—

Thanks for keeping the books, and for
everything else you've done to help me.

On the bottom, I sketched a little pig—
a little portrait of a pig—
and I signed it *Anonymous*.

53.

Tried to see Tiffany today. . . . Stopped by
her house after school. Her grandmother, who's visiting
from New York, was the only one home.

"Tiffany's at the doctor's for an appointment
and some tests. I don't know when she'll be back."

She must be Tiffany's grandmother on her mother's side,
'cause she eyed Blake's muddy feet
the same way Mrs. O'Neill always does,
and as soon as we left, she came outside with a broom
and started sweeping his paw prints off the drive.

Must be nice, though, to know
your grandmother.
I think about mine sometimes—what she looks like,
what I might call her . . . Grandma Speare? Mom-Mom? Nana? . . .
if we ever meet. I wonder if she
thinks about me—what I look like, how I do in school—
and part of me hopes she'll send me a letter to say
that despite everything she's lost, she's doing okay,
that maybe we can get to know each other
someday.

I left an envelope for Tiffany's grandmother to give to her
with some of my sketches inside:

that one of Tiffany on the bus with a pumpkin head,
   a new one of Michael's profile (I thought he'd be mad, but he
      just smiled and lifted his chin when he saw me drawing him),
         and one of Blake stretched out, asleep, on my rug.

I looked for a "get well" card at the drugstore,
but they were all stupid or sappy or dull.
Instead, I put in a note to her that said:

   I hope you're feeling better soon.
   I miss you at school.
   Come over to the farm when you can.

   Love, G.

   P.S. Michael keeps coming by my locker after class.
      What should I do?

54.

Sometimes Blake sits at the door
and looks out, like he's waiting, like he's expecting
someone he knows, any minute,
to walk in.

As I write this, I am sitting next to
a big bunch of purple lilacs
that I picked last week
and arranged on my little nightstand in a coffee can
like you used to. When I first brought them in,
Blake sat right next to me, almost
on top of my feet, his nose twitching,
his tail wagging. (Do dogs have flashbacks? Do they
remember things like humans do?)

Momma, do you remember how just us three—
Blake and you and me—
would walk down to the little stream
behind the trailer park and pick huge bunches of lilacs?
We'd bring them home, arrange them
in coffee cans, and fill the whole trailer
with their sweet flower smell. Then,
when Daddy came home, we'd sit outside
on that rickety picnic bench and eat ice cream—
Blake would get some, too—
to celebrate the coming of spring.

Today, after I'd picked a few,
I gave Blake a bowl of vanilla ice cream,
which he finished in no time flat.

There was enough for me, too, but I
wasn't very hungry. Instead,
I pulled out this diary
from the drawer by my bed
and wrote this down, so you'd know . . .

we have not forgotten.

55.

Daddy got a phone call from
Great-Uncle Doug in Atlanta. It seems he's coming up to
Philadelphia next month for business.
"I'll be less than an hour away," he told Daddy.
"I was hoping I could drive out, just for the day,
and maybe we could get re-acquainted."

Daddy said after you died and all that bad stuff happened
between him and your parents,
your uncle Doug was the only one who
apologized, the only one who felt bad about
what they'd done to you
and to us.

He told Daddy he can't wait to see me,
and maybe if things work out okay,
we can come visit him in Atlanta someday.

I figured Daddy—being Daddy—would say
"Maybe," or "I'll think about it," or possibly "No, I don't think so,"
but instead he wrote down your uncle's number
and told him he'd be in touch
by the end of the week.

Maybe it's me getting older, or maybe
it's his job going pretty good, or maybe it's just

the warmer weather and sunshine . . .
but something inside of Daddy has loosened up—
like the ice on the pond I saw split
apart one April afternoon,
the sharp edges slipping under the surface
until hardly a ripple was left.

56

Mrs. Reed stopped me
in the hall between classes:

"I'm sorry about the other day,
when you came by to get your books
and I couldn't talk to you much because of
Freddie Cromack's nose. Anyway,
I really enjoyed your note—and your sketch, too.
Mrs. Yocum gave me that desk set for my birthday.
She got it at that museum down on Route 1,
where she's a member. You like art, right?
Have you been there?"

I said: "Yeah, I've been there . . . ,"
and before I had to say anything more,
the bell rang and I had to run
to history.

I was almost late for Mr. Hendershot's quiz.
Even though I tried to study for it this morning on the bus,
I couldn't remember which general was where,
on which date in which year,
and who he was fighting and why.
I ended up guessing a lot, but I *got* General Hood—
(I'd read about him in my Savannah visitor's guide).

I finished and had ten minutes left, so I sat there
wondering if Mrs. Yocum was
anonymous.
It *did* make sense: She's not really a teacher,
so maybe the "no gifts" rule doesn't apply. Plus,
she's given me something already (this red leather diary),
and she *knows* I like to draw,
'cause that's pretty much all I did when we had our meetings.

I should probably thank her in person, but I'd rather
just write her a note and sketch her a picture
of a pirate or a pig
or maybe my self-portrait, a big
pumpkin on my head.

57.

Tiffany came up to me after history
(she's back in school for half-days only)
and asked if she could help me
groom and walk the horses after school.

It's been two weeks since she collapsed
on the track in gym class,
and she has had to stay away from

practice,
friends,
the farm,
and full-day school,

and she has to go to counseling
and a teen recovery group. She told me
that at first she'd been taking
pep-you-up stuff from the drugstore—
caffeine pills and cold medicine, mostly—
but then Ronnie Kline offered her some Ritalin,
and when that worked even better, she kept buying it from Ronnie
and using more.

Now she's getting healthy again
(the doctors said she could have wrecked her heart
if she'd kept on like that),
and even though she's not allowed to do sports

for another couple of weeks,
she can start to see her friends again
and take walks whenever she wants.

We sat in the same seat on the bus,
and she got off at my stop,
and we spent the afternoon grooming Ella
and the two new Shetland ponies,
and walking Mr. Kesey's old gelding,
and playing with Blake,
and just hanging out and talking like we used to
when Tiffany first moved in.

I showed her my folder of pencil sketches, charcoal drawings,
and pen-and-inks, the ones I'd finished but didn't
send in to the judges.
We set them all up against my bed, and Tiffany filled out
a little white label with an original title
for each one (actually, I don't like titles much, but Tiffany
had such fun, I couldn't stop her).

So now I have thirteen drawings with Tiffany's titles on them.

"What am I going to do with those?" I asked.

"Don't worry—someday you'll be famous and I can say
I knew you when you were just getting started
and I named all your pictures."

Tiffany is a true optimist. After these past few weeks,
it's good to know that part of her
hasn't changed.

58.

This morning before homeroom, Miss Benedetto
came by my locker, waving a letter,
and pointed me toward her room. The letter was from
the Arts Grant Committee in Harrisburg, and it was addressed
to me. I tore it open and read it slowly, out loud:

Dear Arts Grant Applicant:

We have completed the judging for next year's state-sponsored
Grant 2834-7-B, "Arts Enrichment for Gifted Students."

We received more than 482 applications from your region, and
from that group we selected 100 finalists. From those we chose
50 students whose work we felt met and, in many instances,
far exceeded the necessary requirements:

1) originality of thought
2) masterful use of materials
3) creative experimentation in form, genre, or content
4) overall quality of the work

The judges' decisions were difficult, as each finalist exhibited a high
degree of competency. If you did not make the final list of 50, we
encourage you to re-apply in three years, when we expect to have
additional funds.

Results are posted on our Web site: www.artsgrant2834-7-B.pa.gov
Thank you, once again, for your participation.

Sincerely,

Victoria Collier, Chairperson, Arts Grant Committee

I sat next to Miss. B. while she typed in
the address on her PC. She clicked on the link at the top
labeled "Winners"
and scrolled down slowly through the names
that were listed in alphabetical order, until she came to
"McCoy, Georgia."

This time it was
my eyes opening wide,
staring at something
I could hardly believe.

59.

Tiffany told me what it was like
to go to confession: "You sit on one side of this
little booth, and the priest sits on the other side,
and you tell him everything you've done wrong, and anything
that's been bothering you
since your last confession."

I figured that was as good a way as any
to tell Daddy what he needed to know
before the art show.

I waited till he was in the shower
(he rigged up an outside one with wood sides
that we use when it gets warmer,
so we don't have to use that tiny one in the trailer),
and I pulled up the picnic bench right next to it
so I was sure he could hear me.
I told him

how someone named *anonymous*
sent me a membership
to the Brandywine River Museum,

how it came in the mail
right after my birthday, when he still seemed angry
about my drawing so much,

how I'd been taking
the Route I shuttle bus after school—
once or twice a week—to visit the museum,

how I had tried to learn all I could about drawing
from looking at the paintings
by those three Wyeth guys,

how Miss B. had asked me to apply for the grant,
how I decided he wouldn't like it—even though I really
wanted to know if I was good enough—

how I'd applied anyhow
and found out this week that I got picked,
how I was sorry I didn't tell him before,
and I hoped he'd forgive me,

how I was so glad that he was coming to school,
to the art show, to meet Miss Benedetto
and see my stuff.

Daddy turned off the water, asked me
to throw over his old scruffy robe
(you would remember it, Momma—it's *that* old),

came out of the shower,
and sat down next to me.
"You must think I am one mean S.O.B."

This was supposed to be a confession, so I
stuck to the truth: "No, not mean. Sad.
I didn't want to make it worse."

Daddy got up, went over to his truck,
and brought back your sketchbook.
"Here—this really belongs to you. I'd like
to look at it sometimes, but you should keep it."

When I took it from him, a long brown envelope
fell out. The return address said:
Membership Office, Brandywine River Museum,
Route 1, Chadds Ford, PA 19317. It was the receipt for
my membership, and the postage date
was my thirteenth birthday.

"I'm sorry, Georgia. I've not been
the easiest person to live with. But I'm getting
better, you know? It's getting a little easier now, for both of us,
don't you think?"

I stared at that envelope in disbelief.
As usual, I did not know what to say.
Daddy put his arm around me and hugged me,
and I buried my nose in his scruffy old robe,
and for the first time since the day you died,
we both had a good, hard cry.

60.

Lots more people came to the
Longwood Middle School Art Show
than anyone thought. I had two pencil sketches, one
pen-and-ink perspective, and three "free choice" pieces
displayed in the main hallway. Our work was arranged
by class and grade, with sixth, seventh, and eighth
each having its space.

I showed Daddy my six pieces,
plus Marianne's sculptures and CD covers,
Tiffany's sports collage
(torn magazines and tissue—it's really pretty good),
and Michael Stitt's still life of a fishing reel, rod,
and trout bones (he liked Georgia O'Keeffe after all).
Miss B. talked to Daddy a long time, which I
kind of expected and didn't really mind, but it was

Daddy who surprised me. At first he asked her about
art class and about the grant program,
but then twice when I walked by on my way to the
cookies and lemonade, he was talking about stuff
that had nothing to do with me
or with school—movies, food, and the new commuter route
that the state was putting through.

Miss B. looked real nice
in her white blouse and long blue skirt.

Her peacock feather earrings
brushed her shoulders when she talked,
and her thick black hair was pinned up in back
with a silver clasp. I couldn't help noticing how she
was looking at Daddy, and how handsome Daddy looked,
and how much he was talking,
and sometimes even smiling, with Miss B.

It was real quiet going home—we were
all talked out, I guess. I finished my math while Daddy
stopped at the store to get us something special
for breakfast. He came out with six sticky buns,
a half-gallon of milk, and a dozen
red roses in cellophane. I think I smeared
a whole page of equations
when I read the little white card he'd slipped under the ribbon:

   Georgia—

     I am so proud.

       Love, Daddy.

61

A busy Saturday. Mr. Fitz has entered Ella
in a big show in Harrisburg
tomorrow. He went out there today to scout the competition
and told me to

bathe her,
walk her,
groom her,
braid her mane and tail,
wrap her legs (so they stay clean),
muck her stall,
and bed her down for the night.

It took me from noon till 6:00 to do most of that.
By the time I was done braiding the last bunch of mane,
I told Ella that if she won any ribbons,
I thought it'd only be fair if she'd
share them with me.

While I was locking up the feed bin and pushing the
wheelbarrow with the next-to-last load of
manure behind the barn, Tiffany came running up the hill,
wearing her lacrosse shirt.

"Hey!" I yelled. "Thought you couldn't play."

She caught her breath, explained how she'd gone
to a tournament for the day,
and since she still isn't allowed to play, she'd been the

water girl
stat keeper
snack provider.

"I was *soooo* bored, Georgia, I nearly went
out of my mind. Thought I'd run up here
and see what you were doing."

We went back in, grabbed two root beers from Mr. Kesey's
old soda machine,
and while Ella finished her dinner,
we sat on the hay bales and talked.
She told me about the tournament—
who played and who won and where the teams were from—
and I showed her the program for the horse show
that Ella was entered in.

Then pretty much out of the blue, she said she was
sorry she'd offered me those pills,
sorry she'd lied about Ronnie Kline,
sorry she didn't tell me about all her
sleepless nights and those days when she felt
shaky and half-sick. She was sorry she didn't
let me help her.
"I thought if I could just catch up—
take those pills to get me through a few busy weeks—
and then stop taking them . . .
but then I couldn't stop, and I couldn't sleep.
I thought if I told you

I was buying Ritalin from Ronnie Kline,
then you would worry about whether
to tell or not to tell
and that wouldn't be a fair thing to do to you."

I told her I'd already figured most of that out,
I'd already been worried.

Tiffany said sorry again. She meant it.
She wanted me to trust her. That's what I wanted, too,
but I also felt like testing her.

"If you really want me to trust you again," I said,
"you would grab that other shovel
and finish this mucking."

Tiffany eyes opened wide in disbelief.
She's an athlete, so she's used to
hard work. But she's also used to playing games
on a nice green field, with a uniform and cleats,
and staying pretty neat. She likes the *idea* of horses,
but not what they leave
behind.

I heard her mumble some four-letter words
as she walked into the stall
with the shovel
and finished the mucking.

62

Mrs. Yocum called me
down to her office. She called it my "progress visit."
She wanted to know how I've been doing in school,
if Daddy and me had been talking more often, and if my
stomachaches had gone away, or at least if they were better.
She asked if I thought my diary writing was "fruitful,"
which meant, I guess, did it
do me any good.

This time the rabbit in my stomach was small
(it still kicked a bit, but I mostly ignored it).
I told her I'd noticed from my writing
that I have my daddy's stubborn streak
and his natural shyness, too. Also, I had a lot to say to you
that must have been stored up inside since you died,
and even though I know you can't answer—
that I'm really writing to my memory—
it felt better to talk to you on paper
than not at all.

She blinked awhile behind her big glasses,
then she asked me if I
wanted to keep writing to you
in my diary.
"Probably, yes," I said. "Until June . . . maybe longer."

It was quiet while Mrs. Yocum made some notes in her folder.
I doodled on my binder
and thought about everything that had happened
since the last time I sat there:

getting that membership in the mail,
    spending afternoons at the Brandywine and
sketching like a maniac to get that grant;
    worrying about Tiffany, then patching things up;
finding out more about you and writing down
    what I might ask you if you were here;
Daddy letting go of some sadness, us talking again . . .

Finally Mrs. Yocum looked up,
and with a half-smile she said I'd made "good progress"
and that she'd like to see me one more time
before the end of the school year.

Marianne and Tiffany were sitting outside, waiting.
"Okay, you're next," Mrs. Yocum said to Tiffany,
who rolled her eyes and whispered:
"At least I miss history."

I got a pass to my next class from the secretary.
Taped to her desk was a new list:
"Longwood School District Artistically Gifted Program"—

and my name was at the top.

Acknowledgments

My sincere thanks to the following people, who contributed their expertise and encouragement during the writing of this book:

Joan Slattery, wise and gracious senior executive editor at Knopf/Crown Books for Young Readers; Allison Wortche, editorial assistant; Eileen Spinelli, children's author, poet, and ever-cheerful friend; Jane Flitner, assistant educator at the Brandywine River Museum, Chadds Ford, Pennsylvania; Karen Fuchs Guidas, art teacher, Lionville Middle School, Exton, Pennsylvania; Ellen Crowley and her L.M.S. History Club; Susan Brennan, generous friend and reading specialist at Rainbow Elementary School, Coatesville, Pennsylvania; Debbie and Ariel McManus, volunteer readers; Allison Kohn, LCSW; Lisa Parviskhan, D.O.; and, above all, for their constant patience and support, Neil and Leigh Bryant.

J.B.

Could Lyza's summer mystery lead to . . . pirate treasure?

When Lyza helps her dad clean out her grandfather's house, she discovers an envelope with her name on it. With the help of her two best friends, Lyza must figure out what the enclosed maps mean—could her grandfather really know where the famous pirate, Captain Kidd, left buried treasure?

www.randomhouse.com/kids

A Book Sense 76 Pick

**A Bank Street College of Education
Best Children's Book of the Year**

Life is quiet in Katie Leigh Flynn's New Jersey town. She watches the trains in the railyard with her best friend, Mike, and dreams of the faraway places in her postcard collection.

Then, on a windy night in 1932, a shocking crime shakes Katie's town, and all of America, to the core: the baby son of aviator and American hero Charles Lindbergh is kidnapped from his crib. A manhunt begins, and when Bruno Richard Hauptmann is captured and accused, Katie, only twelve, finds herself inside the courtroom at the Lindbergh baby trial as an assistant to her reporter uncle.

In a suspenseful novel in poems, Jen Bryant takes us inside one of the most widely publicized criminal cases of the twentieth century.

★ "Extraordinary. . . . As Katie says, 'When a man's on trial for his life/isn't *every* word important?' Bryant shows why with art and humanity." —*Booklist*, Starred

"Bryant crafts a memorable heroine and unfolds a thought-provoking tale." —*Publishers Weekly*

"It's not hard to get caught up in the trial itself and in Katie's trials and triumphs. And it's easy to fall into the lyrical rhythm of Bryant's public and private revelations." —*San Francisco Chronicle*

"Readers . . . will be swept along in suspense."
—*The Horn Book Magazine*